AWA.

Now a Bone-Chilling Motion Picture...

dr. phibes

William Goldstein

Based on the
screenplay by
James Whiton and
William Goldstein

The doctors of London were being murdered
—horribly, grotesquely. Each killing
was part of a bizarre ritual based on
the ten curses of the Old Testament...

ORIGINAL "DR. PHIBES" BOOK I MOVIE TIE-IN FRONT COVER
PUBLISHED BY AWARD BOOKS 1971

DR. PHIBES was dead, charred to ashes in a flaming car crash while rushing to be with his wife as she lay dying on the operating table.

Or was he?

The doctors of London were being murdered - horribly, grotesquely, monstrously. The first was stung to death by bees; the next was torn to bits by bats. The third was mutilated with the mask of a frog. The fourth was savagely drained of all his blood.

Somehow the deaths seemed to follow a fiendish pattern, all part of a bizarre ritual based on the ten curses of the Old Testament - *boils, bats, frogs, blood, rats, beasts, locusts, hail, death of the first born...and darkness.*

No one knew why.

No one could stop them.

No one, that is, except Dr. Phibes – a half-dead madman with horrific master plan that has only just begun...

For something that used to be Dr. Phibes was still alive, blood-thirsty for revenge and insanely killing . . . killing . . killing . . . killing . . . killing . . . KILLING

DON'T MISS THIS SPINE-SEARING FILM

Starring

VINCENT PRICE * JOSEPH COTTON

IN

"DR. PHIBES"

WILLIAM GOLDSTEIN

dr. phibes

BOOK I

of

THE CULT-CLASSIC

DR. PHIBES SERIES

dr. phibes

BOOK I

of

THE CULT-CLASSIC

DR. PHIBES SERIES

WILLIAM GOLDSTEIN

Book design by Damon J.A. Goldstein
Copyright © 2013 by Damon J.A. Goldstein
Forever Phibes Icon and book plate design
by Damon J.A. Goldstein
Copyright © 2011 by Damon J.A. Goldstein

Published by Phibes Phorever Publishing

First Phibes Phorever Printing, October 2014
10   9   8   7   6   5   4   3   2   1

ISBN-13: 978-1502848376

Book design by Damon J.A. Goldstein
Cover design by Damon J.A. Goldstein
Art direction by Damon J.A. Goldstein
Phibes Forever Icon and book plate design
by Damon J.A. Goldstein

ORIGINALLY PUBLISHED BY AWARD BOOKS 1971
Copyright © 1971 by
American International Productions (Eng.) Limited

Printed in the United States of America

$$\pi^2 = \infty + \frac{\infty}{\pi} = \frac{\infty}{\pi}$$

Formulaic Hypotitheñai
From The Dr. Anton Phibes Manifestos
- circa 1929

dr. phibes

by

WILLIAM GOLDSTEIN

Based on the screenplay by

James Whiton and William Goldstein

for Dr. Phibes

dr. phibes

Chapter 1

FIRST the pain stopped. It went away. It came back. It exploded.

A siren rang somewhere or should have. Wheels seemed to be racing, rubber whipsawing the asphalt. There was a safety kit in the tonneau cover; could he get to it? But it was locked in the car; where was the car?

The siren should be closer now, its undulant shrill more or less urgent in the violet air. Violet was the color of twilight, always the best time of day. He liked to meet Victoria at Burks for cocktails on Tuesdays and Fridays, her days in town; he tried to get his desk cleared by 4:45 so he could beat the going-home rush. By five the cabs and buses were frozen motionless and the noise along Pell Street elevated out of normal range of civility. Burks was a seaport, its burnished paneling and tile floor providing sufficient reminder that man could still design his days with just the right level of comfort. During March and April, and again in late fall, the light prismed from blue through several stages of violet to purple through the leaded glass windows. The logs in the grating popped as the resin drops surfaced and burnt. Victoria's gloves glowed in the firelight and she was very beautiful then. Yes, Victoria was very beautiful then.

A wave of pain came back again. Sharper this time. Almost as the last wave was receding the pain was on him again—and again, this time before he could take a breath. Then twice in quick succession, like a tuning fork. And once again, as if from memory. Then it came rapidly, sharp and hard.

He wanted to run, dodge off that bloody road; somehow he had to get into the ditch. It was coming again—he could predict it in the memory of the previous pain. Where was the ditch?

He'd left Berne at one: to make Calais by dark he'd have to push. At the time that didn't bother him, partly because he knew the road even though he'd been on it less than half-a-dozen times and partly because his car—an Hispano Suiza roadster—was precision tuned. He traveled eight months out of the year and lived, as it were, by timetable. Rail service was still tenuous after the war, so he'd gotten into the habit of keeping a speed-rated motor car close at hand. The Hispano Suiza was the third he'd bought for that purpose, and its eighty miles per hour cruising speed was something of an assurance. The wooden steering wheel imparted a firm enough sense of the road to allow him to negotiate 45-degree turns in third gear.

Three quarters of the way down the road he picked up a river—at first little more than a small stream—crisscrossing back and forth over it in a series of trestled bridges. On the straightaways the road ran parallel to the stream, which is why he knew the ditch was there.

His head felt like a steel mask cabled by zones of stress. When the pain came—and by now his perception was heightened in the twilight air—he'd be ready for it. As soon as he got to the ditch he would wash himself in the cold water. He thought now how good that would feel, and swallowed as if from some terrible thirst at the imagined touch of water. Then it came again.

Faster now. It was coming faster. Like an alarm bell it rattled and scraped against the layers of his face. The pain now assumed a third dimension. Its edge seared and cut the zones of his featured mask, crosscutting equanimity and surprise, patience and presumption. His very composure wavered, then crumbled in slow motion.

Then he dissolved in a vast implosion of pain. The last reserves of his composure evaporated at impact as the new pain billowed into him, like some Byzantine globe.

Now it knew no bounds; the yellow-orange globe bounced, clanged and rolled about the reaches of his skull, hurtling pieces of his memory past him so fast he started to remember, to forget, in an alternate dazzling switch of pain.

He began to chuckle at the kaleidoscope. The images came into view in a jerky mechanical fashion, hung suspended before a white-sheet backdrop, only to be pulled from sight. The whole show resembled a billboard display tunneled out on sledges by hidden puppeteers.

Then it came again: a rash, brass, glazed, laminated, round, pendulous onion globe in his catcraw skull head clamped by cutting agony.

And again it came, and he went dark.

The car stuck forty-five degrees out of a hedgerow up the road about thirty yards. The road was banked quite properly at that point, and the car had gone off it riding a clean tangent, rolling twice before it came to rest in the brambles. Absence of speed marks indicated the driver's intention of negotiating the turn—a wish precluded by his machine's velocity. The roadster evidenced very little damage and, save for the fact that it was upside down, looked intact and full of race.

Measured about it was a pronounced silence that seems to go with motoring accidents. One sensed that the outraged metal was gathering new reserves of strength to get under way again. Both car doors were open, their leather-pouched armrests lending an air of finality to the car's circumstances. Willows cast ink-blot shadows on the matted meadow above; otherwise the car was clear, flawless and streaked clean by the sun.

Boulders had halted the forward movement of the car and sent a rippling, jarring metallic reaction through the vehicle, which tore deeply into the radiator grill and cowl, sent the doors flying open and would have, had he still been at the wheel, killed the driver.

One half-hour after the sun had passed the meridian, a new noise could be heard. A thin metallic clicking, low in frequency, but sturdy enough to indicate a great tension, gradually building in volume to become part of the beeswarm buzz above the hedgerow. The Hispano-Suiza, of glass, rubber, leather and metal craftsmanship but still a machine, was, like all materials under stress, beginning to react to the unnatural strains placed upon it by the crash.

In the collision the twin granite boulders had gouged a glaring jagged "V" in the car's cowl after it had struck them head-on at fifty miles per hour. The sportscar hadn't traveled very far prior to the collision point, being whipped off the road, as it were, by its own downhill velocity acting now in concert with the forces that rapidly assumed control when the driver was thrown free at the target point. Of course, with no one to observe him, one could only surmise what happened to the driver as he was ejected from the car. At a fifty-mile-per-hour rate of speed he would have first run and then, the forces of his propulsion overtaking him, rolled or slid the rest of the way downhill to a point somewhat below but inside the tangent described by his vehicle. That the car, in fact, slid downhill was verified by the absence of skid marks. The Hispano Suiza had turned over twice, landing finally, its windshield flattened and cowl to the ground, and then, acting as a two-ton sledge, slid the remaining twenty yards into the hedgerow. In its rush it'd torn off everything in its path leaving a crudely mowed strip from the edge of the road down the hillside behind.

Now it lay upended, its wheels no longer spinning,

doors agape and belly to the sky. Dead in its tracks there was something terribly incongruous about the car's new position, its walnut interiors, leather upholstery and chromium-plated dashboard offset by the brambles and gouged turf in a doubly awkward composition. The car did not, could not, would not work again but yet it was not still.

In fact it was clicking, uncreasing, translating the horrific strains imposed upon it by the collision. From the front bumper, along the cowl, fenders, frame, to the trunk and hindmost bumper guards, the toughened steel that had contained the Hispano Suiza through countless accelerations and decelerations, that had weathered storm and sun-baked straightaway alike, was now, if ever so microscopically, metallurgically reacting. At first these groans and clicks were masked by the beeswarm. But as the sun descended further past the meridian and the hedgerow's animal population had either fled the slaughter or been decimated, the creasing and surging of the fine Italian steel rose and fell in marked juxtaposition to the beeswarm.

In part the car frame had been damaged sufficiently in the crash to crack: the Hispano Suiza was literally breaking open. And it was this sound of fracturing metal that added a new measure of audibility to the air above the hedgerow.

The steel gas tank split slowly but truly. It lay tucked hard against the rear bumper, efficiently fitted by hasps at the rear of the frame. Its flat shape was evenly placed on both sides of the axle. It carried 22 gallons of the standard benzine mixtures in vogue at the time for high performance motors. Mountain driving required a relatively high rate of fuel consumption, such that the tank was at half capacity after the car had traveled a scant sixty miles.

But the tank, if it was half empty, was also half full. It lay flat, steel face to the sun; very quickly the fuel was aboil, the trapped air inside the tank becoming charged with benzine fumes. As the pressure inside the tank built up, the tensile strength of the light gauge steel was exceeded, with the result that the tank, overheated and already weakened by the compacted strain of the crash, popped.

Benzine fumes now streamed out, mixing with the pollen, giving it a sickly sweet cast. The beeswarm by now had expended the limit of its fury and had turned its attention to the buckwheat. Their buzzing had quieted sufficiently, so that, had there been someone to listen, he now could have heard the car breaking up.

The fuel tank was split open by a hairline crack that ran jaggedly along its midline. Although the danger of the benzine reaching its flashpoint inside the tank was over, the fuel was now boiling freely in the afternoon heat. As the fumes rose upward in the tank, they condensed against the cooler outer surface of the crack. Soon a stream of benzine was trickling down the face of the tank where it paused to collect in drops at the lower edge before it spattered on the drive shaft below. There the first few drops evaporated, but soon the process was producing enough condensed benzine so that the flow was continuous. The drops of fuel became a trickle, then a steady stream which seeped down the drive shaft to the gear box and thence to the motor housings.

Of course the ignition had not been turned off. It was

only a matter of seconds when the benzine, in all its volatility, reached the magneto. The explosion in the next instant erupted and flashed up the benzine stream where it ignited the remaining eight gallons still locked in the fuel tank. The explosion blew off the back half of the car and sent a shrapnel storm of fiery metal and blazing benzine jets into the hedgerow with such force that the brambles were incinerated for a radius of thirty feet about the wreckage.

The ensuing fire was still smouldering six hours later when it was discovered by a milk wagon driver. The local constable who inspected the site just after sunset, reported nothing but bits of twisted metal in the ashen residue. "Both car and driver were incinerated in the fierce heat provided by the burning fuel," he concluded in his report.

The driver had lain in shock fifty yards down the road where he'd half slid, half-fallen after the accident. The benzine explosion blew him into the ditch. The water collected there from melting snow, literally saving him from death by dehydration. He was to remain in the ditch another day and a night before he made his way across the fields. His name was Anton Phibes.

Two weeks later, some boys from a hamlet at the base of the hill found the Hispano Suiza's walnut steering wheel in a strawberry patch two hundred feet uphill from the fire-scored hedgerow. Miraculously it was unmarked.

Chapter 2

"HAVE some more Chateau d'Yquem, Albert," Lady Palo-fox urged, "its oh-nine, your favorite year. And it was the absolute last bottle the vintner had on his shelves. I literally had to bribe Mr. Swarthout to get him to sell it to me."

Albert Dunwoody half muttered through his mustache. He quickly plugged his mouth with a spoonful of thick turtle bisque and, glowering across a dinner table heaped with food, inhaled the tarragon-and-caramel-scented liquid in palliation of his frayed sensibilities. Rising up like a volcano was a ham of herculean dimensions, its clove-studded sides angrily aglow against the patrician white Irish linen tablecloth that was, even at this early stage of the banquet, displaying the smears and laverings of two dozen hungry guests at its perimeter.

Dunwoody's thick neck prevented his viewing the guests at either side, except, of course, that he had noticed a lady with outsize powdered breasts being ushered to a seat three or four chairs to the right. He would have to look her up after supper. For the moment he'd have to content himself with acknowledging his hostess who sat diagonally across from him just beyond the watercress salad which, lamentably, was reposing in a low crystal bowl. He leered at Lady Palafox who even yet was appraising him through a pair of rhinestone encrusted spectacles.

Albert Dunwoody, M.D. F.R.C.S., Chief of Gastroenterology at London's Guy's Hospital, was in high demand among his clients as a dinner and bridge guest and all-round "extra man." His girth and manner bespoke a fortune which was rumored to be in excess of 100,000 pounds. In fact he had less than a quarter of that on deposit at his bank, much of his estate having gone toward the upkeep of a succession of young Swedish secretaries. Two disastrous mining ventures in East Africa had corroded the remainder of his cash reserves and now he was reduced to living on the income from a practice in which he'd long ago lost interest. As it were, Dunwoody's patients were all middle-aged wives of bankers, industrialists and other new money types whose saccharine diets and love-dry lives provided little more than chronic indigestion and an occasional gallstone to tax his professional ability.

Lecher that he was, he loathed having to cater to hordes of mooning wives, corseted widows and long-since ripened spinsters, but he also knew that continuation of his lifestyle depended on dancing to these ladies' tunes.

It was much worse after dinner. Lady Palafox insisted on doing a recitation: some interminable sixteenth-century piece about a parrot peppered with so many hard consonants that her false teeth clicked in audible agony. She was a thin whippet of a woman, with cadaverous features and a tall onyx-dyed coiffure. She wore a deep V-necked lavender evening dress that exhibited a full half-yard of long decolletage. "A bloody skeleton," he sulked as the lady's ribs rose accordion-like to the poet's meter.

The other guests—a dozen couples whose names could be read in the society columns in any of the London weeklies—reclined in the cavernous parlor in attitudes more akin to postprandial fixation than attention to the lady's dramatic offering. The Skewes-Coxes (Sir Harold wiped his low brows repeatedly with an outsize handkerchief) were in steel. Solly Gildenstern and his creepy Austrian wife anchored one end of a large settee. In press circles he was rumored to be a "comer." Lady Elspeth Gay had made a name for herself in the National Health Service; her husband stood by the mantelpiece smoking a disgusting black cigar.

Dunwoody sloshed some brandy and let his eyes probe the reaches of the large room; anything to block out that damned verse. Now he probed for the lady with the talcumed busts. As soon as the ordeal was ended, he'd bring her a glass of sherry. Then, if could be, divert the husband. . .

Finally, "Speak Parrot" ended, as it'd begun, in a rage of "k's" and "g's" that rattled the sedate room air with unnatural violence. Dunwoody earlier had tried winking and leering at the object of his attentions. With awkward rapidity he grew anxious, aroused, then, decidedly unrequited.

Lady Palafox's concluding barrage brought him to the

edge of his seat, the abrasion of her skewered passion tightening his own. Yes, the old leonine swell had returned to his loins. Could he get up from the safety of his seat? But he had to get close to the lady. They'd meet for lunch tomorrow at Lupsons, and then perhaps a discrete interlude at his apartment. Should he supply flowers or perhaps a little something in jade or opal? No, that wouldn't do: no need to arouse the husband this early in the game. It would have to be lunch for the time being and nothing more. Well, nothing except the extensions of their own felicity.

His heavy loins quickly sobered him. The others were stirring about and if he was to snare his prize, he'd have to make his move now before the bridge game.

He shoved his hand into his coat and embarked down the long parlor, thumbs stuck out dead ahead like a resolute explorer. The other guests were rising up out of their chairs now, still dumbstruck by the verse torrent. They seemed loathe to cross the broad expanse of the floor outright but rather sallied along the narrow spaces between chairs and tables in a sort of dumb ballet. So much had been said so monotonously for so long a time, that there was little conversation.

Dunwoody nodded as he brushed past the first few couples. His flagged coat lapels had attracted little attention. So far, so good. He'd advanced about a third of the way when he saw something that crumbled his spirit. The lady, who'd been sitting alone throughout the recitation, was apparently about to be gathered up by her husband.

"Albert, you promised us this rubber," a voice said in

his ear.

It was Skewes-Cox at his side, and his monstrous wife, billowing like an obese dahlia, moved directly in his path. She was his best patient, he having just concluded arrangements for her annual two-week checkup at a private spa. The woman was as healthy as a pair of draught horses but she was an untiring patient.

"Of course, Henry," he muttered weakly, "I just want to glance at this marvelous tapestry." He started to brush past the Skewes-Coxes when a steely hand gripped his elbow. Without looking he resigned himself to the inevitable.

The doctor motored home in high gloom. The bridge game had been a disaster. Lady Palafox had insisted on rubbing knees throughout, the friction only serving to fire his sense of defeat. To lose at the hands of a rival was a point of honor; to be outplayed by a husband was disgusting. He played fitfully and lost gloriously, consuming half-a-dozen tall scotch-and-sodas in the process. At midnight he escaped only by promising to come again in a month: the thought of having another chance at meeting the lady of his desires being pale consolation for the long grim evening. Of course it was too late to find a companion for the evening, he'd have to return to a desolate bed.

Fastidious gentleman that he was, he seldom availed himself of the women to be found patrolling the streets of London's seamier districts. No, Doctor Dunwoody kept a roster of telephone numbers in his notebooks, a veritable bibliography of delectables the vivid descriptive language of which, had it fallen into the hands of a less sensitive person, would have been considered absolutely prurient. But young women of this class aspire to a precise mode of gentility, and to call one at an. "inconvenient" hour would have been absolutely vulgar. It was home to bed—alone!

Dunwoody lumbered out of the cab and up the wide staircase to his apartments like a man who'd stood long and well at the bar. He fumbled a bit for his keys, then brushed them out of his paisleyed vest and, unlocking and opening the door with one practiced lunge, burst into his fashionable, if somewhat frayed quarters. When he reached the upper landing he probed around his bedroom without turning on the light: it would have been too difficult to find and he knew the floor plan by heart anyway.

A few steps and he was in his bedroom. Out of long habit he threw his cloak and outer clothes onto the silent butler at the side of the bed. Ross, his manservant, would be up at 9:30 in the morning; he could attend to them then. His shoes were the hardest. One of the knots had come undone and he had to struggle with it, the exertion adding to his weariness.

At last he was ready for bed. Perhaps in the smooth sheets he would find some solace. He pulled a night shirt and sleeping cap from a hook in the closet and tumbled into the outsize bed—a beaten man.

A long hour's sighing and settling followed. It was as if the wheezes, groans and whispering of a thousand troubled muscles had been given voice and vent by the sheets. Dunwoody, drunk and abed was like a spring seeking its proper tension. But, weary as the night had left him, he couldn't sleep. Try as he did, the pillows were never fitted together properly, the heavy velour bedclothes hung like the skin of some long-dead animal, even the air in the room possessed a stiff texture like one finds on deep winter evenings, although Dunwoody kept the house at an unvarying 71°.

He turned the light on and groped for the *Times'* crossword puzzle that he always kept handy on the sideboard. He'd work off whatever it was that was bothering him and then get to sleep: he had rounds at the hospital tomorrow at eleven. The puzzle was about two-thirds finished, it being Wednesday and he liked to string the work out until Saturday so that he could go right on to a fresh one. Dunwoody never ceased to wonder at the infinite multitude of puzzle designs.

Ah!, it was no use. The frustration was restoring his weariness. He scanned the page a last time. Triumphantly he slowly began to print number 1 across: a sinner's reward was D-E-A-T-H. Then he swept his bed clean of newspapers, writing pad, dictionaries and other paraphernalia, flipped off the light switch and threw himself back onto the pillows.

The Dunwoody townhouse occupied a slightly off-center position in a square of similar two-story buildings in London's Kensington district. Many professionals lived there because of its proximity to midtown offices. Guy's Hospital was less than thirty minutes away by public transportation, by cab considerably less. Dunwoody's square was similar to a hundred other tiny enclaves built during the past two centuries by practical-minded architects who perceived the need for such islands inside the burgeoning metropolis. It was a quiet, pleasant place with cobbled pavements, narrow sidewalks and neat wrought-iron fencing adding to the general conviction of privacy throughout the square. The houses were all faced in white stucco and brick, kept clean and sparkling by contracted attendants. All of the windows bore polished hardwood shutters, further evidencing the regard which the square's nearly one hundred souls placed upon privacy. It was a quiet place inhabited by people of measured manner and salutary distinction.

Were one to survey this square on this still dark May evening, one would have seen a quietude unblemished by human or animal intruder. It was a clear spring night, a rarity for that time of year in a London grown used to an abundance of fog. The moon's luminosity marked the soft incandescence of the square's gas lamps. Nothing stirred and each of the houses, their shuttered windows quite dark, were left to an unmolested sleep.

The building at Number 18—Dr. Dunwoody's—was the one exception. That building was being intruded upon. Above, on the roof, a cloaked figure stood. What surprised most was that he should look so natural in this unnatural circumstance. Perhaps it was the formality of his appearance. He stood in silhouette against the dusky horizon, his outline sharp and correct like the formal cameos of a century earlier.

Grave and great strength attended his movements as he bent toward a spot on the flat rooftop. He stood angled in tension for a moment, then abruptly lifted up the building's skylight. Then the figure stepped to the side and slid a large bell-shaped container to the open skylight and lowered it into the unsuspecting house. The entire process required less than ten minutes and was executed in velvet, precise silence.

Dr. Dunwoody was a victim of the flesh in his sleeping as in his working hours. He snored. In long groaning swipes he snored. This bellowing had more than once driven an unsuspecting lady from the bed; now it provided a loud fanfare to the events taking place above his head.

The skylight to his apartment led directly into his bedroom. Its opening destroyed the natural appearances of the apartment, giving it a fractured aspect. The moonlight that now streamed in was unfiltered by any glass and angled obliquely over, not onto, the doctor's bed. It illuminated the room in varying degrees of penumbral light, a light which was abruptly blocked off, then equally quickly restored. Of course Dr. Dunwoody did not notice it, but had he been a normal sleeper he might have stirred awake long enough from the draft of chill air to notice this source of the light perturbation within his bedroom.

A four-foot-tall sack presently descended through the skylight, being lowered ever so gently on a thick velvet rope by someone who was skulking out of view beyond the light frame. But wait! It wasn't a sack; it was a cage, cloaked in a heavy cloth in a manner used by bird fanciers to shield their sleeping pets from the light.

To accompany the cage's descent, Dr. Dunwoody emitted an arpeggio of rapid-fire snores and then, proud of his performance, turned over on his side and was silent.

The cage dropped the last few inches to the floor and came noiselessly to rest, sending up a slight waft of dust from the rugs which was reflected and scattered by the moonlight above.

The rope's tension relaxed, then increased again until it rose straight and taut to the skylight. A barely audible "click" announced that the cage's bottom had been slid open. Now the cage glided upward again ever so silently on the velvet rope.

The rope moved, the cage rose. A low squealing entered the diorama. Rasping, it was the kind of pitch one didn't want to hear on a dark night. Then the squealing ebbed and throbbed, forming in volume a presence that could not be denied. Again, the cage shuttered; then the skylight closed, casting the room into a grayer luminosity.

But the squealing was continuing. It was iron hard now, like a thousand midget sirens. Firm and rasping it ran up and down the walls, into the draperies, wainscotting and chambered parts of the ceiling. Loud it droned, pulsing with the heave of the doctor's chest. His chest rose and lowered, his mouth whispering with the sheets. The squealing darkness ebbed and expanded its own rhythm, the two sounds advancing toward each other in a prescribed Doppler effect.

Then they met. And the room burst in an explosive thematic variation of breathing and squeals.

Dunwoody started to snore but gasped instead. The squeals were now hard, staccato emissions that periodically ran together in horrific tearing bursts.

The bed had become a swirling ant hill of activity, its voluminous sheets filled with hundreds of worrying dark shapes. The doctor was wrenched from his sleep into half-dead wakefulness. What he saw sent him screaming: hundreds of starved bats now driven by their already excessive onslaught to more carnage. But his scream stopped abruptly as it drowned in a gargle of blood from his throat.

He lashed out weakly but the bats were all over him, biting his arms and tearing through his tattered nightshirt in a violent wave of wings and teeth. He lumbered up out of the bed, trying to heave the animals off. A few were dislodged and immediately supplanted by others. He struck out again like a drowned fighter, then fell back into the bedding, bleeding in a dozen places.

Now he moaned, croaking hoarsely for his manservant who would never hear him. The bats were relentless now, biting his eyes, lips, ears and throat to get at the major blood vessels. His tongue was bitten in the midst of a shriek, his beard framing a muted croak.

Dunwoody gestured once again, his croaking cry rasped to stillness. The weight of bats compressed his chest, arms, legs into captured inertia. Then he shuddered, his torn throat gurgling, and was still.

A pillow dropped to the floor. The bats would continue feeding through the night.

Chapter 3

"EVERY bloody screwball death is called into homicide. You'd think we didn't have enough to do with a strangler running loose in Bournemouth, widows being picked up by a mail-order creep, and the inspector's wife running off on him like that" The younger of the business-suited men was talking with great animation as the two approached the stair port of the handsome house.

"Yeah, I just heard that myself. Where d'you think the lady is off to?" whistled the other through plump cheeks stuck high on an ornate stiff collar.

"I dunno; Carver told me she went to Egypt, to see the tomb of Tutankhamen. What is it about middle age that makes women so darned restless?"

"Probably their husbands. The old man doesn't miss too many tricks. Have you noticed the way he manages to get up to the library every other day?" The older man winked as they reached the stairs and, moving ceremoniously to the side, gestured for his chief to go first.

"Yeah, she's a bit of a special redhead. I've been looking

at her myself." The younger man smiled.

"You better keep it at that, sir. You know how the old man feels about playing on the job."

"What's sauce for the goose is sauce for the gander. I'm sure Sir John David Crow wants contented men in his department, men sufficiently secure in their footing so that they can carry out any mission with dispatch and integrity." He winked and held the door open. "What have we here, Mr. Schenley?"

"Bats, Mr. Trout." Schenley punched open the door with his fist and he and Trout disappeared into the house's taciturn facade.

The two men were officers of the London Municipal Police Force's Detective Division. Sergeant Tom Schenley was a career officer, his thirty years of service interrupted only by a four-year stint with the Royal Navy.

He'd been an Intelligence Officer on Vice Admiral Sir Roger Keyes' staff and played a big part in the submarine operations in the Sea of Marmora. The story had gotten around that Schenley had been instrumental in the tracking down and sinking of the first dreadnaught class battleship of the war, the *Barbarusse Hairedoin,* but the lid was still on and Schenley's modesty kept him from talking too much about the war.

When he was released in 1919 he assumed his old rank as corporal, declining an offer to advance a grade. He felt much more at home in the ranks than as an administrator. But his talent for detail and great steadiness on cases was always evident. When he organized the detection of a banknote forgery ring in 1922, his promotion was decreed in high circles. This, Tom Schenley accepted with grace and no noticeable change in habit.

He lived with his wife, the former Nan Exley, in an unpretentious West End flat. The Schenleys never entertained socially, his trout fishing excursions to the lake district absorbing all of his free time. But Tom Schenley was a devoted husband—a leather-bound color-tinted portrait of Nan was one of the few ornaments he permitted on his otherwise spotless desk. Mrs. Schenley taught the sixth grade and, from her portrait, was a still attractive woman of an indeterminate age—somewhere between 35 and 50. Her one noticeable feature was a large pouting mouth.

That she attended her husband well was continuously demonstrated by the Sergeant's manner and dress. Robust, large, substantial, solid he was—but not fat. He wore three-button suits of an excellent fabric and tailoring, and he wore them surprisingly clean and pressed for a man of his bulk. For Tom Schenley, at six foot two inches and 190 pounds, was a big man, a formidable man. He was not known to lose his temper, but when the need arose he could handle himself with commendable vigor. During one particularly difficult arrest, he'd broken a suspect's jaw when the hapless fellow attempted to get a gun out of a shoulder holster. Schenley subsequently referred to the man as a "scurvy bastard," and expressed a sense of outraged decency at his breach of rules.

At an age when most men went to seed in a dozen awkward ways, sprouting thick jowls, sagging bellies and splotchy scalps, Tom Schenley had held his own, achieving in his middle years a seasoned good looks that elicited a new kind of stare from the young ladies and an occasional jealous glance from the men.

The sergeant walked as hard as he looked but an eighth-pound of shrapnel had taken enough zip out of his leg to slow him down. His gait was more like an academician's than a policeman's and, in fact, some of the younger officers called him "the professor."

Harry Trout was a young man in a hurry. Barely twenty-two when a dazzling series of detections brought him headlines and grudging official recognition, his brilliance earned him an inspector's badge two months before his twenty-fourth birthday. During the six months since that date, detective-now-Inspector Trout pushed like a man possessed. In that time he'd brought to successful conclusion three major homicide investigations and opened the files on a fifteen-year-old case which resulted in the arrest of a Derby vicar. The prelate's parishioners brought a lengthy petition attesting to the man's saintliness but Trout's meticulousness linked the man with three spinsters whose deaths had puzzled Dulwich residents a decade and a half earlier.

What Trout had especially liked about this case was that these ladies, the youngest of whom had been 67, all had been sexually assaulted, if such can be said of women of superior years, before they'd been dispatched. Also no evidence of a straggle attached to the crime, and each lady had succumbed in an attitude of bliss, even excitement. In fact, the yellowed photographs portrayed the victims, decked in lace and ruffles, lying abed in truly licentious abandon, not at all in keeping with their station in life. Their deaths would have been attributed to the natural transport that is said to accompany such excesses of the flesh, had not some enterprising patrolman insisted on a forensic check. This demonstrated that, although the ladies enjoyed themselves in a fashion which can be called rare at that time of life, they could not overcome the effects of zinc cyanide. This substance was found in liberal and sufficiently deadly quantities in decorative boxes of chocolate-covered marzipan, several pieces of which the poor dears had innocently ingested.

Trout had theorized that his killer was a genteel, even reserved man whose attenuated sexual appetites were whetted by the peculiar combination of kindness and cruelty, a dual motive that charged many of the religious reformers of the 16th and 17th centuries. Trout further theorized that his man was of a spirituality sufficient so that, if he was not a man of the cloth, he was possessed of deep aspirations for that life.

In a shrewd but obvious (to Trout at any rate) next step, he surveyed local parish birth and death records. The Derby congregation which had been under the tutelage of its new vicar for less than two years, experienced a loss of eight of its elderly women parishioners over that span. Trout's probing determined that three of their number died in the hospital, one had succumbed in a rest home from a long-standing but obscure disease. Of the remainder one had been abroad at a spa for the mineral baths when the end came, the other three lived alone in modest apartments of the kind not-quite-impoverished types take refuge in during their declining years.

Trout had called on these ladies' neighbors and found that they had received few callers other than delivery boys and the Vicar.

Examination of two of the deceased demonstrated to all but Trout's surprise that cyanide had done the ladies in. A local chemist supplied the clincher: the Vicar had purchased the lethal white paste to deal with a "rodent invasion" that descended on his vicarage. The arrest that ensued did not expand Harry Trout's popularity but it added another bright star to his lustrous trail.

Still, the publicity attending the Vicar's case did not help his career. At some point thereafter, high administrative councils within the police department decreed that Trout should be reassigned. In their wisdom they attached to his responsibility a veritable bibliography of more routine matters: burglaries, embezzlements, and an occasional "questionable" death.

Sergeant Tom Schenley had been selected to work with Harry Trout. Schenley's steadiness, his reserve, his unobtrusiveness were supposed to be "levelling" influences on Trout. At the time of their visit to Dunwoody's apartment, the two men had worked together for three months; it was not yet known who had affected the other more.

The inside of Dunwoody's place was clean without being ostentatious about it, attesting to the understanding care of Elihu Ross, a gentleman's gentleman who'd been with the building over twenty years, serving under three different masters during that period. The furniture was old and, although not cheaply made, was well worn; since it had not yet been dusted, it was somewhat musky this May morning. White antimacassars on the sofa and chairs and the bright linen draperies accentuated the quietness of the downstairs rooms. Over-all the air was pungent with the thick sweetness that comes from large amounts of new blood.

Schenley and Trout paced evenly along the black and white tiles, their heels clicking garishly in the hallway.

"Bats you say?" Trout wrinkled his nose. "They're not local hereabouts. What the hell are they doing loose in London this time of year?"

The two men reached the staircase and paused at the heavily burnished post. "From the smell of it, I'd say they'd been feasting, sir." Schenley tapped his nose with a finger and nodded upstairs, "It's up there."

The men went up shoulder to shoulder, their shoes muffled by the black rubber runner. The muted sounds of an investigation in progress could be heard on the second landing. Trout spoke in a measured, clipped tone, "When'd the call come in, Tom?"

"About 9:30 this morning, sir. A fellow named Ross, the valet here, called. Gaithers took it, said the man was near hysterical on the telephone; that he thought he'd gone off his head. Gaithers sent two men out right away to get the valet under control. When they got here, they found the deceased and called in the laboratory people." Schenley glanced at his watch. "They should be finishing, sir," said Tom.

"Good, I hate having to walk around people." Trout looked about the second landing, a spare narrow hallway with two doors leading off, one of which was partially open. Schenley nodded toward the open doorway. As they brushed past a vase of pussywillows, Trout recalled a nursery couplet, something about birds and bees singing in the spring. He gritted his teeth, then followed Schenley into the room.

Dr. Dunwoody's bedroom looked plainer, smaller in the daylight than it had at night. It was indeed a small room, being hardly twelve feet across, a size necessitated by the over-all narrowness of the house.

The room was nearly filled by an outsize bed. Its only other furnishings consisted of a tall "silent butler" at the foot of the bed, a nighttable and a breakfast tray; the last item having been brought in by the valet.

Dunwoody's coat, shirt and trousers of the evening before hung on the wooden butler, rumpled, out of place in the daylight. Trout was amused at the two balled red socks that lay tossed at the "butler's" feet.

"The old goat must've been somewhat irregular," he thought. "And there's something else: he was wearing suspenders and a belt. Now that's a sport for you!"

Trout scanned the room slowly, noting the closed windows, the simple lock on the door, the ornate gas mantle chandelier. Then, his notations completed, he permitted himself to look at the bed.

Under ordinary circumstances that item could hardly be avoided in the narrow austere room: the sheer bulk and festooned coverlets dominated, even dwarfed the area. Now, however, its white expanse displayed such a surgical, such a bloodthirsty chaos that only a man accustomed to viewing life and death in its grossest violence could view that bed with equanimity.

Trout's report read like a pathologist's summary: Albert Dunwoody did not die quickly but lingered in deepening coma interspersed with fits of wakefulness. The bats (three hundred and eighty seven were counted in the room) had descended on him while he lay asleep. The first attack appears to have been so severe that, although he did wake up, he was too shocked and too weakened to pull the covers over himself. That would have been enough to save his life, for the bats were tiny, only three-to-five inches in length, and could not have torn through the bedding. But from that first onslaught, Dunwoody's ability to defend himself diminished. He did manage to dispatch a few of his attackers but this was more as a result of his rolling atop them as they fed on his flanks than from any offensive blows with his fists.

Undoubtedly, Dunwoody tried to shout for help. When found, his mouth was open and contorted. But the bats had torn his throat, probably in the first wave. His throat gorged and pharynx scissored, the victim's voice was stilled in the last few hours of life. Although his esophagus was clogged with blood, Dr. Dunwoody did not die of suffocation, as might be construed from the evidence. Rather it was shock, of a prolonged and cumulative nature, that killed him. As noted earlier, the victim did not die immediately but lay in a twilight state of animation for a few hours before he finally succumbed. It appears that this penultimate period of existence contained a particularly bizarre sequence of events.

Bats are not carnivorous by nature. But like any other animal, they can be driven to eat anything by long periods of enforced starvation. The bats that entered Dunwoody's room were voracious beyond containment. They stormed the victim in a rush that must certainly have appeared to be a vengeful cloud; however, it should be considered that they attacked to feed, not to kill. After they'd torn and gouged enough chunks of flesh and bits of blood, they retired to the curtains and eaves about the windows, momentarily sated. A few stragglers who had not gotten their fill stayed behind to gouge and feed at the victim's now exposed trunk.

Dunwoody's body was covered by an unnumbered mass of teeth marks. In addition to his ripped throat, there were long slashes on his skin where the flesh had been torn out, down to the bone. These gross wounds, some half dozen in all, appeared to have occurred as follows:

The victim fainted after the first onslaught. The stragglers feeding on his skin must have caused new islands of pain. These stinging bites were enough to bring him out of the faint— only to view with horrific realization that he was being fed upon. He writhed and lashed out in an effort to get rid of his tormentors. His wounds, although at this point not major, would bleed anew: the musk of these new freshets of blood drew the bats a second time. Like a cloud, they descended from the draperies striking at exposed and already weakened segments of Dunwoody's flesh.

This process was repeated five or six times, with the victim falling into a deeper and deeper faint after each sortie. An hour of this was about all that he could bear, the resultant coma at least providing numbed relief. Even then he was not able to lie still, his torn nerves causing him to jerk about. These were his most pitiable gestures; for even in his condition, he attracted the violent bats. Each rolling heave of his body, blind and insensate as he was, brought new clouds of the bloodied animals flocking to his wounds. At times literally covered by the furry beasts, he would roll and wallow in an agonized dumb show, the blood running from his wounds, filtering through the clusters of bats that hung on him like grapes.

Alternatively he would emerge from the coma—and the shock of what he saw and felt during these brief flights of consciousness eventually, and all too slowly, killed him.

Trout was able to transcribe his report almost directly from the notes he made that morning. He recalled being both disgusted and enthralled when first viewing the evidence; disgusted at having been relegated to such a patently crazy case and enthralled, even excited, at the prospect of digging into a case that was so far removed from the ordinary. He wrote clinically, quickly and well, and, as was his habit, spoke little in the process.

Schenley was somewhat less taciturn. He questioned the laboratory technicians about fingerprints, bits of clothing and other clues: their search had turned up nothing. Then, taking note of the breakfast cart, its pair of poached eggs staring up lugubriously from two squares of soggy toast, he asked one of the policemen in attendance to summon Ross, the valet. Then he busied himself aiding the other patrolman to sweep up the gorged and by now drowsing bats.

This was accomplished by the simple expediency of tapping the draperies, onto which the animals had clustered, with a broom handle and then sweeping the droppings into large burlap bags. The bats apparently did not like to be thus disturbed and thrashed and squealed about in a somewhat glutted fashion once inside the bags.

"No! No-o-o!!" a man's thin shriek shattered the room's grim composure.

"Now, now, it'll be all right. The Sergeant just wants a word with you." The patrolman half-pulled, half ushered the valet, Elihu Ross, into the room. Ross was a spare, gray man, still in morning uniform. He huddled against the bedroom door, loathe to enter.

"Mr. Ross, is it?" Schenley said.

Ross, distracted, looked up, catching sight of his erstwhile master in the process. He blanched and, pushing his hands to his anguished face, pleaded to be taken away. "I can't look at the master again . . . those things . . . those awful creatures . . . they were all over . . . let me get away from here . . . aaagh, it was horrible!" He moaned and slumped against the patrolman.

Trout waved him out: "Well, d'you think he could have done it?"

Schenley glanced at Trout, puzzled. "Did what, sir?"

"Did in our doctor friend here." Trout gestured with his pencil. "Hey, that's no way to remove him. At least cover up the remains, in the name of common decency." The technicians put down the stretcher which contained Dunwoody's rather garish corpse long enough to restore its modesty with a sheet. Then they conveyed their white-shrouded burden out the door.

Trout and Schenley were now alone in the room.

"You know, Tom, what a butler does best?" Trout continued with a hint of a smirk.

"I dunno, sir. A messy scene, this, but it looks quite like an accident to me. The victim was probably a hobbyist of sorts. What d'you call it: an aviarist. Yes, that's it. An aviarist!"

"But where are the cages, Tom? All pets need their cages. Now you didn't see any downstairs and neither did I. The little buzzards must have come from somewhere." Trout rolled his eyes about the room in mock search. "Aha, there we are!"

Waverly followed his chief's gaze up toward the skylight.

"That's where they came in," Trout now concluded, a hint of triumph in his voice. "And they didn't just fly in."

"No, the skylight's closed," offered Schenley.

"Closed, opened, and closed, Mr. Schenley. The bats were brought here by someone and put into this room via that skylight to carry out an objective for which they'd been prepared in advance."

Schenley was puzzled. "You are suggesting this was planned, sir? But bats? In London? At this time of year? Why and who would want to do something like that? And for what reason!"

Trout again looked at the skylight, this time somewhat archly. "I suspect the murderer will develop that information for us, Mr. Schenley. Let's get it from him!"

Chapter 4

THE man sitting at the dressing table was thoroughly preoccupied with his work. The table was large and oval-shaped; in front of it was a large mirror framed by lights, the kind of mirror actors use to perfect the exact shadings of their makeup.

The man rubbed the area where his nose was supposed to be, applying an adhesive with a small buffing brush. Then he selected a nose, a slightly hooked one, and placed it on his face with practiced skill, using a pair of tweezers. He drew on a mouth with a few well-placed brush strokes. During the process the man kept looking at himself to measure the effect. He tweezed, brushed and shaped each portion of the makeup, dabbling in the creams and powder boxes on the table.

He spent a lot of time with his hair which was thin and lay close to his head. The hair was of very fine texture, the kind one sees on dolls sold at the better shops. It was streaked with gray which required considerable dabbing of a thick dye. He was quite vain, rinsing and brushing the dyed portion several times before he was satisfied.

When he had finished, he towelled off the excess liquid and gave a flourish to his hair with a brush. Then he looked closely at himself for the over-all effect.

His face was oval, somewhat elongated. His skin was mauve white. His eyes, large and filled with despair, dominated. His mouth evidenced a permanent smile. He wore a tuxedo topped by an immaculate white cravat. He appeared to be readying for a special event. From somewhere in the house a waltz could be heard and the man paused for a moment, listening.

He finished his work with a flourish, dabbing, touching and patting the final elements of his makeup. Then, his serene smile a question mark in the mirror's reflection, he backed softly away from the dressing table and arose. He picked up a brocaded dressing gown and hung it in a closet.

The gown was deep wine silk, padded, and very heavy to ward off the cold. Thin black stripings ran up and down the sleeves; at the cuffs, the gown was piped and fluted in marvelous arabesques that represented, on close inspection, the letter "P." This same letter was repeated in raised gold calligraphy on a pair of onyx cufflinks that protruded below the cuffs.

The man was small, condensed in stature, almost frail. His hands were pale and opalescent, their delicateness counterbalancing the ferocity of his eyes. He looked terribly weary and old beyond his years. He held his head to one side, preoccupied by his thoughts.

The waltz music could be heard again. It was Strauss, a

song for graduation balls, tea times or afternoon soirees, certainly sweeter times than this.

The music was filtering along a hall that, despite its elegance and decorum, cried out for people. The carpeting in the hall was grand, a thick robust rose; gold urns atop Corinthian pedestals decorated the ochre walls with ferns and palm fronds. Paintings in gold and rosewood frames soared to the ceiling. A family appeared to be depicted here; hard-eyed men and furtive, voluptuous women, dressed in the styles of centuries ago. At the far end, above double doors, towered the family patriarch—a tall warrior standing at full height in the distinctive armour of Cromwell's Ironsides. His portrait was framed by a gilt construction thicker and more elaborate than that of the others; centered on its base the letter "P" stood out in fine script.

The man in the tuxedo walked down the hallway without looking at his ancestors. He followed the music to its source, pushing open the double doors of the room from which the sounds came.

There, in a ballroom of crystal and gilt opulence, a cluster of musicians, their hair slicked down and their mustaches trim in music-hall fashion, serenaded on a little dais. They were very intent on their music which now poured forth in full glory, inviting and supple. The man crossed the glass floor in quickening paces. He was alone in the ball room; surprisingly, there were no other guests.

But wait—suddenly he was met by a startlingly beautiful young woman whose white ball gown was accentuated by raven hair spread over her shoulders. The man paused in front of her, bowed, straightened and looked at her intently. Then he flicked his hand to the base of her neck, and swept her out onto the floor.

They danced well together: he moving in great strong sweeps, she following his lead with exotic, almost stiff, deliberation. Still no one else appeared. The two seemed perfectly matched and equally perfectly alone above the glass squares. His hands and feet kept excellent time to the beat, his patent leather shoes marking the waltz patterns on the shining surface.

A long swirl brought the couple closer to the dais where the musicians could be seen more distinctly. The players postured stiffly, instruments held at fixed angles, feet keeping time in unison, eyes beady, smiles fixed in plastic teeth under brush moustaches. Could it be? Indeed, yes, they were mannequins. A mechanical orchestra! How novel, how utterly correct for this man to install such realism in his home: a formal ballroom with an appropriately dressed orchestra, high mirror-lined walls that provided infinite reflection for a trio of crystal chandeliers, the brilliant glass floor that stretched to all corners of the horizon.

The music ended and the couple glided to a small cabaret table placed against one wall. A single red rose rising from a fluted glass vase was its only decoration; two bentwood chairs stood around it. He held one for the girl to be seated, then plucked a champagne bottle from a waiting ice bucket, popped the cork and poured two tall glasses. He offered one to the lady; they toasted and drank, she brushing the glass to her lips, he pouring the entire tumbler into a small aperture in his throat.

She remained unruffled by this startling gesture, continuing to sip her wine and look at her escort with deep, yet rather glazed eyes. He sat placidly, unmoved by her beauty, the silence, or the multimirrored reflections. His desperate eyes were elated now, their excitement hiding the despair about him.

A different kind of party, signifying the advent of May, was in process on tailored grounds somewhere near the great city of London. A tall Maypole had been hoisted on a little hillock and two concentric circles of young men and women were moving in opposite directions around it. Each of the dancers carried a long colored streamer, the other end of which was attached to the top of the Maypole; they were making their way through a series of nursery songs in fitful fashion, their singing broken by bursts of laughter. Other couples, mostly in their 20's and 30's, stood before the yews and boxwood. Small tables dotted the lawn. Seated at these were couples engaged in the more serious pursuits that come natural to a warm spring evening. Other couples were clustered along the sweeping balustraded stairway that led into the main building. The stairway—consisting of some 150 steps in all— provided a focal point to the formal gardens which spread out in all directions at the base of the stately home.

The whole place was an island not ten minutes from the Thames and Central London. Linking the two worlds was a macadam driveway that looped into the grounds from the main road. Hidden most of the way by trees, the driveway circled gently up to the house and then out again.

Cars—cabriolets, curtained Landaus and sleek Stutzes—had been gliding softly up this roadway all evening to discharge guests. A canopy of brightly colored Chinese lanterns had been erected to spotlight the new arrivals. These, sporting a dazzling variety of animal masks over jewelled gowns and snowy tuxedos, were treated to applause or laughter, depending on the inventiveness of their creations. Lions, tigers, cobras, lizards and bumble bees lined the stairway as a flowing orange sportster zipped up, its three pairs of chromed exhaust pipes throbbing with the power contained in its engine. Its driver, attired only in a black tuxedo, leaped out over the door as the attendant whisked the car down along the driveway.

The man who now stood tentatively on the cement was youngish and good-looking. He glanced petulantly at the crowd on the staircase, annoyed that they didn't notice him. Apparently he'd neglected to bring a mask, perhaps thinking he could obtain something suitable at the party. He pulled a silver cigarette case from his pocket and lit up. He looked expectantly around, then began walking, his shoulders square and cocky.

Suddenly, before he'd walked more than a few paces, a long silver-gray saloon car eased open one of its doors and emitted a velvet-hatted and elegantly cloaked figure. The man who glided out of the grey plush interior moved with a dancer's elasticity. With a genteel flourish, he swept open a package held with gloved hands, and, in a single motion, extended a squat and bizarrely bug-eyed frog's mask at the walker.

"For that froggie who would a-wooing go!" The walker beamed. He grabbed the frog mask from the cloaked gentleman and placed it over his own head, much like a crown.

"Point me to the women, my good man." The walker clapped his hands with relish, executing a little two-step in anticipation of the night ahead. His amphibian mask gave him a churlish, even ludicrous appearance, highlighted all the more by the elegant black tuxedo draping his tall frame.

The cloaked gentleman looked at the French-windowed balcony above and put a calming hand on his new-found friend. His features were partly obscured by a contoured, smoked-glass opera mask. He was small but of great presence, his hands shaping the air before him. He turned to look at the Chinese lanterns.

He was wearing his usual fixed smile—the master of the letter "P," the man with the strange crystal ballroom, had also come to this event.

He adjusted the clasp at the base of the frog's head, then pushed the younger man toward the staircase. His generosity concluded, he pulled a gold-covered walking stick from the car and stood eyeing the festivities above. By now enough guests had arrived to line the staircase with a complete zoo of masked figures.

Froggie edged his way through the crowd at the base of the staircase, nodding and blinking at a full blouse or a narrow waist. The mask had given him a new freedom and he intended to make the most of it. He stopped to ogle a prize specimen whose heroic proportions welled-up in near nakedness from a leather archer's costume. But Friar Tuck, who hovered at this female Robin Hood's elbow, drove the rounder off.

The man with the frog's head hopped onto the staircase, but he'd only walked up a few stairs when he grasped the base of the mask as if to loosen it. Gaining relief, he hopped up another half dozen steps only to stop again, this time to clutch at the wooden halter.

The others looked down on him, their curiosity aroused.

Froggie climbed a few more stairs, this time staggering noticeably. The other guests appeared to attribute this to the champagne and ignored him when he barged upward in a final burst. Besotted gentlemen were becoming common.

The man-frog was breathing heavily now, clawing and clutching at the unyielding mask in a futile effort to relieve the tightening compression on his skull. He gasped and stumbled about, smashing at the wood with his fists. He screamed in anger. Then in terror. And screamed once again.

This time the crowd was attentive. They looked at him with the dumbness people always seem to muster in the face of tragedy. They ogled and leered through disguises now grown obscene.

The orchestra thrummed a tango. The colored lanterns blinked in the wind. The cypress trees loomed in the darkness below.

The man with the frog's mask stumbled, screamed again, his scream disappearing into an awful dying choke.

He straightened, then stumbled, falling the length of the staircase.

When the others got to him, rivulets of blood from his burst skull trickled grotesquely from the frog's eyes, ears and neck. The man was quite dead.

The police arrived a few minutes later. By then the driveway was clear and most of the guests had returned to the house. A butler and a gardener guarded the body. The saloon car that had carried the original owner of the frog's mask was nowhere in sight.

"Goddamn it, no!" It was not yet nine a.m., an unhappy hour by anybody's yardstick, a seamy, unpleasant hour on this particular May morning when the thermometer outside Sir John David Crow's window had already edged past the 85-degree mark. It was an unusually hot morning, portending a day of frayed tempers for Londoners used to better fogbound air.

"You know better than to ask me for men when we're spread too thin as it is," Sir John continued.

He threw some coffee into a white china cup and gestured for Harry Trout to take some. Trout complied, then renewed his gambit.

"But don't you see the significance, sir? Three medical men have died, each under more peculiar circumstances than the others. And in each instance animals were involved." He sipped his coffee, eyeing his chief furtively over the edge of his cup.

Sir John David Crow, London-born, Oxford-educated, was 59-years-old and looked every inch the patrician. His bald head was ruddy and polished from a good steam bath after a go at the weights; he'd refused to bow to the day's heat, choosing instead to wear a pink high-collared shirt and a red tie that added to his floridity. Sir John, as Department Head of the Homicide Division, commanded a force of some 400 officers and men whose job it was to prevent and control crimes and to apprehend the transgressors. Some 3,500 murders, assassinations, criminal conspiracies, kidnappings and other acts of violence were visited on London's citizenry each year. These crimes and the resulting pain, misery and fear formed the cornerstone of Sir John's profession.

The two men had been talking for less than ten minutes. Sir John had been forced to listen to Trout's much-too-cool dissertation (that was always the way with the young smarty pants). Now Sir John was about to lose his temper and looked like the very devil for it.

"It's too consistent, sir, too damned consistent; if you could let me have liberty for a week, we would put it all together. . . ."

"A week! You've had three bloody days, ran poor Schenley's legs off all over the bloody city, and what've you got to show? I'll tell you what: a goddamn menagerie— frogs, bats, bees; next you'll be telling me somebody's slipped an asp into some old lady's tea cakes!"

"But there's a link, Sir John. A few more days and I can show it to you. After all, they were all professional men." Trout reached for more coffee but was cut short by Crow's bellowing.

"Doctors die every day without our making martyrs out

of them. If you want a plot, I suggest you read Aesop's Fables. That should whet your ample imagination, Mr. Trout."

Trout collected himself and exited as quietly as possible under the circumstances. Just as he was about to shut the door, Sir John fired a parting blast. "Remember, your weekly report is due Friday at noon. And leave that damned zoo out of it! If you're on to something, I'll thank you to stay with the facts."

Trout was still smarting when he walked back into his office. It was a small but scrupulously clean place with high wooden walls, two filing cabinets and a large map of Greater London on the wall opposite his desk. Tom Schenley, his collar wilted from the heat, sat in a cane chair beside Harry Trout's desk.

"You look like you've been through the mill, if I must say so myself," said Schenley.

"Mr. Schenley, during my short time in this department, I've experienced the vicissitudes of obscure cases with little or no clues, of reticent witnesses, fashion plate barristers and brilliant criminals. I've had to answer to friends, family and a juristic system that seems, sometimes, to offer more succor to the perpetrators of crimes than to their victims. I've further endured the scorn of so-called public opinion, but I have not yet, sir, grown accustomed to being shouted at, denigrated, debased, yes, outright verbally abused. And I do not now appreciate it particularly from one whose station and education warrants a more seemly attitude." Trout gave full vent to his ire.

"You mean the old man handed it to you?" Schenley asked.

"He is not an old man but rather a remodeled, iron-seated, rock-visaged, crease-browed, irascible, florid, ungentlemanly, callous, short-visioned, intemperate martinet. And I wish the man would hear me because it needs to be put into the record!" Trout slammed into his seat, threw his feet upon the desk and stared hard at the map opposite. Schenley leaned forward, his arms on the desk. "I take it he has reservations about the case, sir?"

"He told me to go read Aesop's Fables," Trout spat.

Schenley stifled a laugh. "That doesn't sound hopeful, sir."

"That's a euphemism. And the pattern's as clear as the skin on top of his head." Trout glared at the map again.

Schenley attempted to comfort him. "Like my dear wife says: 'Tomorrow will be better.' Besides it's too damn hot today to do much of anything."

Now Trout looked at Schenley coldly. "If it's not done today, we can forget it. He wants it wrapped up by the weekend. What've you got so far?" He nodded at some manila folders on his desk.

"Not too much, sir." Schenley began thumbing through the folders as he talked. "Each was a medical man of considerable standing. Dunwoody, for example, was an anesthesiologist, published a few papers, served on advisory boards and had a pretty good practice to boot. Thornton, that chap up north, did a lot of work with the blood vessels. Came down here a lot as consultant."

"What was it that put Thornton away?" Trout shot out.

"Bees. Somebody dumped a hive into his bath. Hargreaves, the one at the party, was a cut-up. Three wives, each divorced after a year. Social register. Fast cars. Boating. Horses. And women coming out of his ears. But Hargreaves was nobody's fool: top drawer all the way. On the staff of three leading hospitals. Even attended seminars on the continent and in America." Schenley blinked his eyes in conclusion. Then he went on. "But they all had something in common."

"If you tell me each died of violent causes, I'll shove you out the window, you bloody hypocrite," Trout growled.

"No, sir. All were professionals. Each man an individual and a gentleman in his own way." Schenley toyed with his words.

"Come on out with it," Trout demanded.

"Vesalius," Schenley offered.

Trout blinked, then grunted: "Vesalius!? What the hell are you talking about? Vesalius was a 16th-century anatomist!"

"And a 20th-century London specialist," Schenley added.

"In God's name, does the man have an address, a place where we can call on him?" Trout was excited.

Schenley was cool: "We'll be talking with the man in one hour. I've already made an appointment. He's busy but he will see us."

"Busy, hell! He'll see us now or I'll subpoena the bloody bastard."

Trout jumped up and grabbed his coat.

Schenley followed. "On what grounds, sir?"

Trout pulled him out the door. "On the grounds that it suits the crown. Now let's get to him before he changes his mind!"

They dashed out of the room, Trout hatless but with composure fully restored. Schenley grabbed his files and followed Harry Trout who'd already raced halfway down the hall.

Chapter 5

THE Wabash Cannonball roared down the rails at full throttle, white steam hissing in authoritative jets, steel tires clashing, its locomotive blazing across the landscape.

The overnight express thrashed through a grade crossing on its way to Louisville. The string of freight trains had changed this small crossing into a transcontinental exchange: the packed carriers zipped past, shooting grain, coke, truck parts, sulphuric acid, ball bearings and Finger Lakes wine to mid-American distribution points.

The Wabash calaboose sped on; red lights flashed their warning and the crossing gates lifted.

"Dr. Vesalius!" The voice that called seemed to be coming from afar.

Up ahead the Broadway Limited streaked around a curve, diesel churning. Its twelve sleek cobalt-colored cars glinted against the slag hillsides. Each car was emblazoned with a name—Coshohocktin Valley, Susquehanna, Allegheny, City of Vincennes—the brass name plates running the length of its side. To the rear, the sculptured windows of the salon car spelled out the importance of this fast train.

Both trains sounded warning whistles as they headed for an intersection—the Broadway Limited rushing west to Chicago, the Wabash freight highballing south. The express snaked behind some low hills, doubling, then trebling the reverberations of its wheels. Just beyond the bills the freight droned closer: collision course!

Imperceptibly, a switch enervated the track ribbon. A razor-edged segment slid to the left on oiled bearings, activating another pair of rails, another route. Seconds later the freight was angling off onto a small upgrade. Its caboose clattered over a bridge just as the Broadway Limited's diesel passed beneath.

"Well done, Dr. Vesalius," approved the distant voice.

The man on the floor grunted. He checked a stopwatch, made a notation in his manual and looked up.

"Steam is still better than the diesels," he said. "There's nothing rolling today that can beat the mallet." He squinted up from his work, then returned to his notebooks. He wrote with an accountant's hand, the webbed pages attesting to the care and precision he put into his work.

"I hear they're putting electric locomotives onto the Simplon Orient."

Vesalius scowled: "Rubbish. Those tin cans could never make it through the Vosges, let alone the Carpathians." Then he looked up. "Say, who the hell are you anyway?"

"Schenley, sir. I called you earlier. And this is Detective Inspector Trout."

Trout was preoccupied with the trains. "Why Tom, I didn't know you had it in you. You must tell me more about it sometime." He bent to adjust a mobile crane.

"I'm sorry, Inspector, I insist that no one else touch the equipment. It's built to precise scale, you will note, and is quite finely adjusted." Vesalius bristled and watched carefully as Trout pulled his hand away from the crane. He clambered up from the floor as he spoke. Standing erect, he showed a strikingly boyish figure for his fifty-eight years. His large eyes were unkind, even predatory, behind steel-rimmed glasses. His face was long and weathered, matching his lean angular frame. His brown curly hair was just beginning to show some gray streaks. Although it was past ten in the evening, he still wore a black business tie neatly pinned by a single pearl to a slate-grey-and-white striped shirt. Over this he'd selected a linen-belted jacket of the kind karate experts effect. Perfectly creased glen plaid trousers and freshly polished wing-tip oxfords completed Dr. Vesalius' dress.

His living room, in which the three men stood, completed Harry Trout's impression of Henri Vesalius. It was a large, pure-white room, its floor packed with a fabulous array of railroad hobbyist's equipment. A white leather Eames chair rested on one side of a thin glass table whose etched squares held a futuristic chess set. The chess play showed white to hold a decided advantage. Two prints, both by Piet Mondrian, enlivened the wall opposite.

Trout was impressed and found himself wishing the doctor would offer him a seat.

"Of course," Vesalius said, "you've come on business?"

He stared at his two visitors owlishly. He was cool and almost reserved, a manner fashioned from decades of being visited upon by professionals and laymen from all walks of life who sought him out for specific advice on an insurmountable variety of health problems. For Dr. Vesalius was widely and highly regarded as an authority on internal medicine, a distinction he'd fully earned in his practice.

"I thought you'd be of assistance to us, Doctor."

"Come to the point, Inspector, would you?"

Trout's difficult day began to wear thin: "Three men, all belonging to the medical profession, have died during the past week. More than coincidence seems to be at work; your interest could provide important assistance."

Vesalius cut him short: "I'm not much interested in the medical profession any more, Inspector." He looked about. "After awhile, other factors come into play."

Patience completely eroded, Trout's words came clipped and measured: "Do the names Dunwoody, Thornton and Hargreaves mean anything to you?"

Vesalius blanched. "Of course, we all worked together at one time or another. What are you driving at?"

"Just this: they're all dead, each one in a strange, ugly manner. I'll tell you what we know. And then I'll leave it up to you to decide if you can help us."

Vesalius was finally impressed. He flicked the "off" switch in the remote control unit he held in his hand, stopping the rail traffic at his feet. Then he sat, mandarin-like, on a stack of bright pillows, motioning Trout and

Schenley toward the portable bar at his left.

While Trout recounted the somber details of a case still in formation, a new segment was about to be added which, if not illuminative as to motive, would certainly stimulate public notice.

Chelsea then, as now, housed the coming, not-yet-arrived artists who, having been drawn by the big city, found a measure of hospitality and comfort in its worn buildings and well-used shops. Rooms there rented for 18 shillings a week, and included a hotplate, a sink in the closet and at least one grimy window to let in a bit of daylight. The shower down the hall, which yielded hot water for one hour each day, easily balanced out the convenience of the rent. And, if the warmth of one's quarters was somewhat lacking, the streets abounded in opportunities for meeting a new friend, a contact, or, if the fates were willing that day, even a lover.

To other Londoners, Chelsea was a bazaar. People came there to see and be seen. The well-to-do called it slumming when they ventured out to visit the fashionable coffee houses of the moment. Later, they would come alone, for different, more private reasons. Social service workers and university people also spent many evening and weekend hours there, ostensibly for research. Matrons came by the afternoon busload, lured by Bengalese woodwork, Korean tin kitchen-ware, dried kippers from Iceland and Greek ginger. Evenings they queued up at bus stops, feet aching, their net sacks packed with booty, anxious to make their neighbors jealous with talk of shopping exploits. Their husbands could be found on the same Chelsea streets during lunch hours; they would drift from bookshop to bookshop in fervid search for risqué maidens and dervish dancers, catapult artists and lady acrobats or other sumptuary themes. These booklets, more popular than any best-seller, were bound in unobtrusive covers to prevent detection by blue-noses on the Vice Squad.

For the visitor, Chelsea tried—and succeeded for the most part—to cater to all tastes. For the people that lived there, it became an easily worn shield against the rough handling of the outer world. Its plain restaurants, of which there were many, offered thick beef and fish soups for two pence and one would get a boiled hambone covered by a thick layer of potatoes and cabbage for twice that. At the coffee shops, one could find any kind of conversation—from military preparedness lectures to first-person accounts of life on the Wyoming trail. On special occasions, a passable pilaff could be enjoyed along with a bottle of resinous sweet wine at one of the numberless East Indian restaurants.

Wesley Longstreet had just returned from one of these establishments and was now leaning on the railing of the stairs leading to his second-floor rooms; he was exhausted. It wasn't from physical exertion that Longstreet was now gasping but rather because he'd overeaten. He allowed himself one good meal per week, on Wednesdays, and tonight he'd chosen the East Indian place. The pilaff with skewered lamb had been quite enough but he'd gone overboard on the sesame cookies. He really couldn't help it, for his own attempts at the saucepan had turned him into a drudge and ruined his palate to boot. He hadn't had any warm food since last Friday when the scrambled eggs and kidneys overran on the stove, and ignited and blackened the closet wallpaper.

Now Longstreet grabbed the rail and pulled himself up the remaining steps; he groped down the murky landing to his door, only to fumble at the doorlock. He'd forgotten his key or at least he couldn't find it in the myriad pockets slit into his waistcoat, sweater, vest, or trousers.

He grew desperate. The wine had done its work well and the new discomfort was reaching an intensity sufficient to have him hopping about the hall.

Mercifully, the ancient door, its brown-green varnish chipped and iron-hard with age, wheezed open.

"Why, it's Dr. Longstreet."

He rushed past dear Mrs. Frawley, his landlady of these past seven years, and raced to the tiled sanctuary next to his bedroom, pausing just long enough to edge the door closed in the name of modesty. But had he been able to hear over the watery din, he would have been mortified at Mrs. Frawley's unwanted audience.

He washed his hands with a bottle of green soap borrowed from his office, scrubbing his nails and wrists in the practiced manner of surgeons. For Wesley Longstreet, despite his idiosyncrasies, was a practitioner of that medical art. Indeed, Wesley Longstreet was a member of the Royal College of Surgeons and enjoyed the honor of those few colleagues who knew of his work as well as the respect of his students.

Had Wesley Longstreet so desired, he also could have had a considerable fortune and all the embellishments that go with it. But Dr. Longstreet was from an early age in the medical profession. Dedicated to the principle that quality medical care should be obtainable by rich and poor alike, and noting that for every physician that practiced in the city's working class districts one-hundred others had established themselves in the West End and other fashionable areas, he made the simple personal choice of living by his convictions. Had Wesley stemmed from a conventional family, he would have created a stir, to say the least. But his father had been a labor organizer, travelling extensively about and eventually dying in the Midlands. His mother maintained the household, raised three children, and helped keep bed and board together by working as a vocal coach.

Causes were not lightly treated in the Longstreet family. Wesley's decision to pursue medicine was met with determination, his decision to serve the poor, with acclaim.

But temperaments of that depth are not usually simple things. Wesley Longstreet had an exotic streak in him as well, camouflaged but not otherwise corrupted by his missionary spirit. If he couldn't quite live with the poor, he'd live near them. When he'd settled in Chelsea seven years earlier, it was more out of this well-concealed exoticism than out of convenience, although his tiny office in Cheapside was a few minutes away by tram.

Wesley never paused to acknowledge that he himself

was far removed from affluence. In fact, the word "comfort" could not even be applied to his financial condition. For Wesley Longstreet, burdened still by debts incurred in setting up his practice and peppered daily by pleas from his patients for pocket money, lived a hand-to-mouth existence. Whatever spare money he could accumulate he sent to his mother for her keep; otherwise his habits closely approximated the Spartan ethic.

But although one could not tell it with the naked eye, Wesley was not lacking in his pursuit of pleasure. Further, he was certainly not the kind of man to deny himself once he'd found it. That he'd found it and that he was going to enjoy it was the second reason he'd rushed back to his apartment after dinner.

Wedged between the pharmaceuticals and bandages in his physician's bag was a reel of film. And newly packed on the reel was twenty minutes' worth of Natasha doing what the bookseller had described as her "sizzling terpsichorean interpretation." Wesley had even been privileged to glimpse a preview (he was an old customer) of Natasha in the privacy of the bookseller's cloakroom. One look at her bare rump convinced him that the film was worth every penny of the pound the man was asking. Glasses still steamed, he threw the crumpled note onto the counter and ran out. He was still running by the time he'd gone the six blocks to his apartment. Now his hands were shaking in anticipation as he dried his face with a towel.

"I'm leaving, Dr. Longstreet. See you in the morning!" Mrs. Frawley's voice crackled in that sing-song way of hers.

Wesley grunted; his eyes were full of soap.

"How's that, you say?" she wailed through the door.

Would the witch never leave? He glowered in the mirror, his face still red and raw from the green soap.

"Dr. Longstreet! Are you all right?" her voice slipped closer. Now she was tapping on the door. He'd have to get rid of her personally. With extreme effort, he fixed a smile on his features, dabbed back his stringy hair and advanced toward the door. Then he opened it and prepared to address the woman who was his charlady, fairy godmother and tormentor at times.

He caught himself short. She was wearing a daisied hat, a coat that almost looked new, and bigod, a plunged neckline that, in the face of the massed wrinkled front it offered up, was absolutely indecent.

"Where the hell are you going?!"

"Why, Dr. Longstreet!" She'd never heard such an utterance from her dear charge's mouth.

He blushed and tried again, much more in character this time: "What I mean is, Mrs. Frawley, please have a good evening wherever it is you're going." He tried to move past her.

"I have a rendezvous with a social acquaintance. We're going dining, Doctor." This said, very sweetly, she turned and, mustering a bit of spring to her ancient kneecaps, plowed toward the door.

When she was finally gone, he tiptoed into his parlor where he'd slyly thought to set up his viewing apparatus the evening before. It was for his medical research, he'd explained to Mrs. Frawley when she looked quizzically at the small hand-driven projector and silvered screen. Now it stood silent, wintry, and disgustingly mechanical.

He pulled the cover off the projector and set about threading the film. Despite the fact that he'd been collecting these lascivious treats for several years, he'd never learned to properly operate the requisite equipment. It either ran too fast or too slow, it became overheated or the screen, usually at some inappropriate moment, would fly up to his great horror. Worst of all, he could never thread the film properly and spent several desperate minutes winding, removing, rewinding and inserting the celluloid.

But this night things went smoother than at other evenings. The film went in on the first try, much to his amazement. His body heat rising, he pulled a brandy bottle and large snifter from a desk drawer, adjusted his easy chair at what he thought to be proper viewing range and, flicking the overhead lamp off, readied himself for a first taste of the pleasure.

As was his habit, he viewed each new acquisition four to six times, depending on its quality.

With each viewing, he consumed an equal measure of brandy to sharpen his senses and prolong the effect. He poured his first glass now and started to reel the film.

What he saw on screen kept the promise of the bookseller's cloakroom. Natasha, long of limb and full of grace in every soft curve, leapt out from behind a colonnade and began a throbbing, sensuous series of dance steps the like of which he'd never seen before. With each variation in pitch from an unseen orchestra (which Wesley imagined to consist of drums and reeds), she discarded a veil. Now he could see her navel, properly jewelled, now a rosebud or two above, equally dazzling, now even her arms turned like snakes about the colonnade, her hips sweeping back and forth like an angel's broom. Would she ever take the remaining veils off?

"Dr. Longstreet!"

"Good Lord, she's back," Wesley thought in panic. He stopped the machine, but not before the wretched charlady had descended upon him in full flower.

"Why, Dr. Longstreet, why are you sitting here in the dark?" She looked at him with piercing fish eyes from beyond the screen.

He fought for control. "Just some research, Mrs. Frawley. Did you forget something?"

That seemed to satisfy her.

"I just came to get my gloves," She turned and walked out.

It scarcely bothered him that she might have caught him. As soon as he heard the door close, he started reeling again, this time more feverishly than before in a hurry to get to the "good" parts.

Natasha was emerging again from behind the colonnade. And there they were—two ripe full breasts that stood free and clear from her magnificent torso. But she was not yet still! Now she arched and flexed her hips in a rotating compression that set the firm buds above into a rotating motion. This vision of compact flesh reacting to muscle control was more than Longstreet could bear. He sipped deeply of his brandy, letting the frame hold on its magnificent vision.

Then he set to reeling again, more slowly this time, taking in every aspect, every motion of the tremendously organized Natasha. He drank again, and then again, toasting the revelation before him.

Longstreet's senses were clogged now with gelid desire. It is doubtful that he could have heard the door of his bedroom open, more than doubtful that he could have done anything to prevent a gray-cowled figure from sneaking up close to him and, then, in a dazzling instant rendering him unconscious with a compression blow to the base of his ear.

In a single reaction Wesley Longstreet slid backward in his chair and on the way out of life. To complete the action, the figure slipped a gloved hand about the brandy snifter, removing it from Wesley's languid grasp to place it carefully on the floor.

Then, fixing Natasha in a pose of innocent abandon, he repaired to the bedroom. When he returned, he carried a physician's bag similar to Longstreet's and a large black oilskin satchel.

This he laid open at Longstreet's side and removed several vacuum bottles, laying them neatly in a row about the doctor's feet. A small motorized pump came next, which he set up on a side table wheeled next to the easy chair. Working quickly now, he pulled a roll of rubber tubing from the oilskin and, attaching one end to the pump, affixed a long needle to the other end. Then he expertly located a heavy vein in Longstreet's arm and inserted the needle into it. He led a third length of tubing into one of the vacuum bottles, bent swiftly to his physician's bag and removed a pressure cuff.

With chilling precision, he placed the cuff on Longstreet's arm above the needle, inflating the cuff with a final stroke which sent the blood coursing from the hapless doctor's body.

His work finished, he stood back to watch the pump take over. Soon one bottle was full. He readied a second, placing the first quart of blood on Longstreet's mantelpiece. As he returned to his station, a small brass amulet dropped to the carpet, snapping off from a chain about his neck. It was the Hebrew symbol for "blood."

While the third bottle was filling, Wesley Longstreet awakened. But he was too weak to do more than look in helpless shock at the man who was murdering him. A few more movements of the pump and Longstreet lapsed into unconsciousness again.

The man removed the bottle, replacing it with a fresh bottle and, moving with the grace of a battlefield surgeon, put the filled container on the mantelpiece next to the others. He repeated the process four more times, then finished, removed his equipment and left as silently as he had come.

Later that evening, a call reached Inspector Trout at Dr. Vesalius' house. He took the news of the fourth victim quietly, almost as if he'd expected it.

Chapter 6

"THAT arrogant sonofabitch! I've heard of professional reserve before but this is outright gall. The cheek of that man: four of his colleagues, men he's worked closely with over the years, are murdered and he thinks he *might* be able to help us." Schenley shook the phone and slammed it into the receiver.

"Tom, the good doctor will hear you." Trout looked at his partner with an amused grin. "That's no way to talk to a member of the concerned citizenry. Now tell me what he actually said."

Schenley still frowned. "He hung up on me, said he didn't like his breakfast disturbed but that he'd give it some thought and get back to me in a few days. He could've at least faked a bit of concern . . ."

"Well, now, sergeant, you have to consider the 'professional' mind. A cool manner, devious in thought, an insistence on priorities and attention to details. These are society's Brahmins who defend the right to privacy at all costs. Concerned the doctor most probably is; he just didn't want you to know it."

"I still say he's a cold, stiff bastard. Give me a bloody amateur any day." The telephone rang again. "If it's who I think it is, I'm going to let him have it," Schenley said; he listened for a moment, then glared at Trout. "The charlady just came in."

"Let's go!"

Trout drove all the way to Chelsea without saying a word. Schenley could tell the case was beginning to get to Trout from the way he negotiated the traffic. The Inspector seldom drove when he was working, preferring to take in the scenery, mapping out his next step in the battle while the countryside zipped by. The only time he actually drove was when he was restless or when he knew exactly what he was going to do.

"Why should they do it to him? The doctor never meant anyone harm. He was such a good man. Oooh, ooh help me!" Mrs. Frawley sobbed into her hankey. She still wore the daisied hat, slightly drooped, and her valiant coat of last evening. The shock of her charge's death had thrown her into such disarray that her gray hair, uncombed since she arose, now lay damp and matted about her face, providing her with a skewed and slightly waterlogged halo.

Trout patted her on the arm and then continued: "Did Dr. Longstreet have many visitors, Mrs. Frawley, anybody that came here frequently?"

She shook her head, moaning balefully into her knotted fists.

"What about family, did he visit them often?"

"He sent his mother a bit of money whenever he could." This recollection of filial piety sent the woman into new fits of sobbing.

Trout looked about the room for some distraction, then glanced at Schenley, who acknowledged his plight. The inspector patted Mrs. Frawley on the shoulder and pursued his questions with great forbearance.

"Could he have had any enemies?"

She looked up from her handkerchief, her red-rimmed eyes flashing anger now. "Yr befoulin' the memory of the most generous man this town'll see for a good many years. He lived for his patients, cared for them day and night, went out after 'em in all kinds of weather; they gave him gratitude and little else. Poor's they were and to him."

She nodded at the ashen corpse of her benefactor who, still in the seat of his last night's pleasure, dominated the room with glazed stare and eternal smile.

"They were his whole life." She hesitated at this new sense of remorse. "May the ones that done this to Dr. Longstreet burn in hell for their sins." Her courage collapsed with her shoulders and she was wracked with heavy sobs, groaning and wailing with such violence that Trout led her into the other room.

When he returned, he paced quickly about the room, then addressed the victim directly with a trained clinical eye. He checked the fingertips, neck, eyes, teeth with practiced precision, looking for powder burns, discolorations, edema, and finding nothing. Then incisively he rolled up the left shirtsleeve and straightened the arm out at the elbow, remarking in a quiet, even tone: "That's how he did it."

Schenley looked up from the draperies where he'd been probing. "Umm, oh yes, he's really quite dry, sir. Wouldn't you think he could have stopped it? I mean, one just doesn't submit to this sort of act."

Trout inspected the puncture mark on Longstreet's arm, speaking deliberately as he was thus occupied: "Whoever did this knew what he was doing. He used a pressure cuff— the skin creases up above the puncture mark—and used it with diabolical efficiency if I may editorialize. It was a vacuum pump, as witnessed by the rings on the mantel top. He took seven liters out, which is all the body holds, in less than twenty minutes. You can check me on it, but my guess is that's optimum speed for a quarter-horse motor!"

"But twenty minutes, sir—how can you specify that span?"

"Because our friend here was wrapped up in his home movies. I'd say his taste ran more to the Little Egypt genre than anything else. That reel runs twenty minutes and he hadn't quite finished."

Mrs. Frawley had tiptoed back into the room and now stood meekly at the threshold, looking for all the world like she'd just emerged from under a shower. "Will you be needing me for anything else, Inspector? If not, I'd like to go back to my own house."

"Of course. Go home and have some warm tea. If anything comes up, we'll call on you in a few days." Trout turned in relief to Schenley: "Tom, help Mrs. Frawley to the door and see that one of our men takes her home. She's been most helpful to us."

Schenley took the dear lady from the room, his heavy frame shielding her damp frailty.

Once he was alone, Trout renewed his study of the victim. He stood before Longstreet, hands folded across his chest, thumb pressed to his lips, balancing on the balls of his feet. This was a mode of concentration he'd developed in college. To grasp the full dimension of an object, to *perceive* something rather than merely see it, he would look at it from a distance. Although he was city-born and bred, Harry Trout was an expert on trees, having already published a series of papers in *Nature* on the most serviceable plantings for urban environments. He'd taught himself about trees by the simple expedient of looking at them, first from distances, then through closer inspection. He'd probe the bark and lower branches with his hands, his fingers gauging the strength, suppleness and age of the wood.

Harry Trout carried this fastidiousness into his social life. He never met people, he observed them. The simplest handshake was a ritual, an ornate composite of hints, false starts, oblique motions. Had the recipient of his observation been able to surmise Trout's intent, he would have withdrawn his hand immediately. But Trout had long since learned control: his motions, on the outside, were affable, studied, contained.

He was conducting an organized search now: shaping, adding, removing bits here and there. By the time Tom Schenley returned, there was little Trout did not know about the mechanics of the murder scene.

"I'm done here, Tom; what have you got?"

"Not a helluva lot, Inspector. Just an old lady's remorse." Schenley put his hand in his pocket. "Oh, yes, and this little item."

He pulled out a brass amulet, holding it in his palm for Trout to see.

"Where'd you get that, Tom? It's an amulet of some sort. If my Hebrew serves me, the symbol for blood."

"Over behind the mantelpiece. No prints: it appears to have been dropped at random."

"Not at random, Tom! By accident is closer to the mark. That belongs to our man." Trout was firm in his declaration.

"Do you think Longstreet's killer is the same man who did the others in?"

"Think it? I'm certain of it."

Harry Trout had a new kick to his walk, Schenley noticed, as the two men dashed down the front stairs to their car. Some children were playing punch ball in the street and Trout dashed off the curb, grabbed the ball and gave it a vicious swipe with his fist. The kids went howling down the block after their toy.

"I didn't think you had it in you, sir, and it's not even lunch time."

Trout motioned for Schenley to drive, then hopped into the car on the other side, slamming the door.

"Thanks for reminding me, Tom. Let's find a place with some good boiled beef and horseradish. We can check the telephone book there."

"For metalsmiths?"

"Now you're getting to it!"

It took them thirty minutes to find a reasonably quiet place with a telephone. Thirty minutes of stop-and-go inching through streets clogged with trucks, cabs and crowds of people rushing to eat and get back to the office. But it was worth the trouble: the thick beef chunks they were served were pink and rare inside, the rolls were fresh and there was enough ale to wash it all down.

The telephone directory yielded six custom metalsmiths in all, two close at hand, the remainder spread far enough away so that they'd have to hurry to get to them before closing time.

Dudley Knightson's was the first stop, a small shop that occupied the top floor of a threestory loft building. Except for a cardboard warehouse at ground level, the loft was all but deserted. They climbed the three flights with no thought other than to hope the staircase would stay together long enough to get back down.

The Knightson establishment was another matter and, under different circumstances, would have been worth the special trip. Once they'd gotten past the receptionist, a wizened male clerk who must've doubled as bookkeeper, they were propelled into a gigantic room whose endless reaches occupied the full top floor. The room was crammed with women, women who otherwise would have worked as seamstresses or chambermaids. These ladies stood at long iron tables in the centers of which were stacks of the most fantastic assortment of stars, wheels, balls, snowflakes and other ornaments. The women were daubing these with paint: blue at one table, red at another, yellow, green, purple at still other stations. Other women rolled tall tray carts about, of the kind one finds in bakeries, collecting the trays of ornaments as they became ready at the long tables. As the carts became full, the ladies wheeled them toward the rear with a great clattering and rumbling. There a rough drying area had been rigged up—double lengths of sheets stretched between four upright posts and beneath outsize bulbs in the overhead lamps. The trinkets baked there before being packed and sent off to gift shops, to be snapped up by an army of housewives who, seeking a way out of tedium, had turned to "home decoration."

"A toy factory in broad daylight is an infinitely depressing place," thought Tom Schenley. He was about to nudge his chief to leave when a bird-like little man descended on them from behind a cart. The man rained such a torrent of high-pitched words that Schenley was stopped before he could pull Trout out the door.

"Gentlemen, gentlemen, gentlemen, welcome to the Dudley Knightson establishment, designer and manufacturer of the finest quality artistic metalwork in England and the continent. Been in business for a century-and-a-half and our name is known by persons of sense and sensibility the world over. Now you've seen the artists at work; I'd like to show you the fruits of their handicraft and, if there's any special item required to brighten up that special wall at your home or office, you can count on us to have it in stock. I'm Dudley Knightson VIII and who do I have the pleasure of talking to?"

The man looked at Trout and Schenley, both of whom stood frozen beneath the frenzy of his introduction. Finally Schenley coughed into his fist and hazarded an answer.

"I'm sorry, sir, we didn't come to buy."

Knightson's torrent began again without pause: "That's all right, that's all right. I'll be happy to show you our artists anyway. They take great pride in their work and have done so many beautiful things. . . ."

Trout cut him off.

"Mr. Knightson, my name is Trout and this's Sergeant Schenley. We're with the police department and we'd like you to tell us about this if you can."

Knightson squinted at the amulet, then fluttered his hands. "Cast brass, cast brass, we work with sheets, just sheets, gentlemen. More pliable, more flexible for our medium. That's a casting."

"Who might make something like this?" Trout turned it around in his palm.

Knightson was unflapped. "A casting, a casting, who will do a casting? Benedicks? No, no, no, they're too big. Kifferstein, yes, Kifferstein; they do very good work. They're in Germany. Very old firm. Highly respectable."

"Isn't there something closer to home?"

Knightson zipped right on. "London, London he wants. Jason Bowditch. No, he's dead. Wife went off and left him so he shot himself. Who else . . . let me see, what's the name of those chaps that do the ceremonial cannons? Gunderson Brothers. Big, old, substantial military concern. And there's that jeweler fellow, not far from here, he is. Does some work in brass but I think he's retired. Let me see, what is his name? It's Italian, I'd recognize if it I saw it."

Knightson threw his hands up to assist his memory. Trout and Schenley, sensing an opportunity at last, made the best of it and eased out past the mail clerk without taking leave. The little man was still chattering when the doors closed.

Simone Latto's place, in contrast to the bedlam which they'd just left, was as quiet as a monastery. Trout and Schenley had little trouble finding the address; the building was located in a nest of small shops stuck behind a long row of brick-and-wired-glass factory buildings. The shops apparently had been spared by some builder's oversight and now attracted the area's workers as well as visitors who came to lunch at the local Italian restaurant.

Trees had been put up in the cobbled square and although the area was crowded, the thickly leaved elms and sycamores absorbed much of the din of conversation.

Harry Trout admired the way the sycamores had been pruned. Each major branch had been clipped at the same spot repeatedly and the resulting wood knots, as thick around as the trunk, shot up clusters of slender branches, each one in bud. Trout spotted the building they wanted. He called to Tom to follow him and they set out across the square.

When they reached the place, a pleasant two-story yellow stucco-and-wood frame building, there was no outward indication of what went on inside. Only the street number gave them reassurance that they had reached the right spot.

"Odd, isn't it? D'you think we should go in, sir?" The sergeant seemed a bit wary.

"We'll never know if we don't, Tom." Trout led the way along a trellis-covered entranceway. Morning glories twined about the lattice overhead and their multi-colored blooms had attracted sparrows and a few hummingbirds. At the end, the solid wooden door was shut tight. They knocked and waited.

"Better give it another go, Tom." Trout thought he heard some activity on the floor above.

Schenley tapped again, louder this time. They waited; still no answer. Again he banged, this time with a full fist. They were just about to try the lock when a gravelly voice boomed through the wood.

"Momento."

Inside the stairs clattered and the door was wrenched open by a huge patriarch who stood scowling at them from beneath thick, scruffy eyebrows, "What you want?"

"I'm sorry, sir, we're looking for a metal-works shop," Schenley replied.

"I'm Latto," the giant growled and, turning around, walked back inside the dark interior. Trout and Schenley followed Mr. Latto into they knew not what.

They certainly were not prepared for what they found inside. There, in a large gallery-like room at the front of the building, was the most fantastic array of brass angels, globes, helmeted warriors, stainless-steel ceremonial urns, steel and brass firebirds, brass-inlaid shields, turtles, twin lions, squat cylindrical brass owls and other emoluments. Each piece of finely worked sculpture was arranged on a series of pedestals, tables and wall shelving; towering above the whole display were two giant stainless-steel madonnas that shot up to the ceiling. A small inscription, "Facit Simone Latto" ran across the base of each.

Latto led them through a narrow hallway toward the one other room on the ground floor. A few steps and they'd emerged into a spare, bright workshop whose whitewashed walls and high windows gave great spaciousness to the room.

A small forge and bellows were located along the rear wall. Work benches lined the side walls—stacked along the tops and shelves of these were the heavy mallets, shears, punches and chisels of Mr. Latto's art.

He ushered them to a rough bench, then lumbered over to the forge and bent to inspect the firebed. Apparently the heat had dropped too low. He folded the bellows in his huge hands, getting up a good stroke until the forge was roaring gently. When he turned to his guests the sweat was streaming down his arms, darkening the rough, leather ironworker's vest he wore against the sparks.

"What'che want?" he growled.

"Mr. Latto . . ." Trout began.

"How you know my name?" he cut Trout off.

"I've seen your work at Marlborough. You're perhaps the most acclaimed metal sculptor living today."

Latto brushed away Trout's words. "Why you come here?"

Trout pulled the brass amulet from his pocket and held it out for the old man to see. "Did you make this?"

Latto answered without hesitation. "Sure, I make it. Ten pieces in the set. About two years ago!"

Trout was surprised. "Ten you say, in a set?"

"Yeah. All different. It's Hebrew."

"But who ordered them?"

Latto thought for a minute. "No one ordered them. It came by mail. A list of measurements."

Schenley perked up. "Hebrew. But if nobody came here, didn't you worry about getting paid?"

The old man blustered at this slight to his pride. "Pay me? They sure did. Nobody works for nothing. It came by mail. And it was a pretty good fair price too—a couple hundred pounds."

"By mail, you say? What about delivery?" Trout queried.

Latto smiled. "Oh, that was a pickup. A young girl, very pretty. She came in. Didn't look around, just took the package and left."

Trout continued the questioning. "Was that all there was to it—ten Hebrew symbols commissioned by mail?"

Latto scowled. "No, whoever brought it make sure he get originals."

"How do you mean that?" Trout interrupted.

Latto went on. "Well, with a casting you just pour metal into mold. You can make more pieces, all the same. This person make me break the molds!"

Trout was surprised. "Break the molds?"

Latto nodded. "Yeah, break the molds and throw them away like he don't trust me."

"Would you have more?" There was a wink in Schenley's eye.

Latto threw his arms open. "What for? Nobody buys alphabet letters."

Schenley started to laugh. Latto began to quiver, then worked up into short bursts, finally exploding into great gusts of laughter. He roared and howled about the letters and the perfidy of the customers, jeering and alternately damning the people on whom he depended for a living. Finally he finished, gradually keying down like a heavy ostrich about to land. Then he was able to speak again.

"Say, you boys make me happy. How 'bout some grappa?"

Schenley started to beg out, "It's late in the day, Mr. Latto. I think we'd best not."

But Latto would hear none of it. He lumbered over to a tall cupboard, dragged open the door and produced a heavy wickered carboy and some dingy cups. These he placed on a workbench and, uncorking the carboy with a solid "thung," began to pour the grappa.

"Grappa's good for the bones. Puts iron in your skeleton, makes you fight better. Here, drink."

He held out two full cups of red wine. Schenley glanced at Harry Trout who grabbed one of the cups and raised it up in a toast.

"I propose we drink to all those lovely men and women out there." He gestured with emphasis. "Men and women who, but for their softened tastes and fattened pocketbooks, would not be able to provide the fundamental bridgework on which all great art rests. Glory to them, gentlemen."

They drank, the grappa curling Trout's throat with its strength. Then Simone Latto started to laugh again. He was still laughing when he let them out of his shop into the softened afternoon.

Chapter 7

"SHEMA Y' Israel, Adonai, Elohenu, Adonai, Echod."
The congregation resumed as one voice in this great prayer
of Hebrew unity. The men, some fifty in number wearing
silvery-white tallis over their dark business suits stood
before hard wooden benches on the main floor of the small
Sephardic synagogue. Their bass and baritone chants rose
up to mix with the lighter tones of the women who,
according to the orthodox custom were in the balcony,
separated from the men.

A young lad held forth on the small lectern this fine
Saturday in May. He was flanked by the rabbi, a substantial
gentleman whose curly brown beard flowed out over his
outsize tallis, quivering with the resonance of the prayer.
The cantor, a shorter bald man who dominated the chanting
with a piercing tenor, loomed at the boy's left. His father and
uncle, both beaming in familial pride at the boy's entry into
manhood, waited at the rear of the dais.

The boy's voice rose loud and clear above the others:
"Boruch, Shem K'Vod, Malchuto, L'olam, V'oed." The

congregation followed his lead, "Boruch, Shem, K'Vod, Malchuto, L'olam, V'oed," their voices surging throughout the small white and wood-paneled room. A row of narrow, colored-glass windows admitted the thin sunlight, staining it into red, green and purple diffusion, bathing the rows of men and benches on the main floor in unaccustomed softness. Twin nine-tipped candelabras guarded the approaches to the arc at the lectera's rear, their eighteen burning candles condensing this soft light with prismatic effect above the lectern.

Harry Trout had come into the building at a climactic point when the cantor was about to open the arc. Trout was confused at first with the chattering cadenced voices. The men seemed to be speaking at random which, for one unaccustomed to the service, came close to cacophony. He'd come purposely to see the rabbi, Ezra ben Gabirol, without realizing that his old friend would be officiating at a Bar Mitzvah this Saturday morning.

The chant ended and the men around him stood silent, waiting expectantly. Now the lad turned and, with firm steps, led the others toward the arc. He opened the covered wooden doors with a firm hand to reveal to all who were in the congregation that morning the blue velvet-jacketed scrolls contained therein. Then he faced the audience and, his features set in new conviction, enunciated again the great principle:

> "Shema Y'Isroel, Adonai;
> Elohenu, Adonai Echod."

With that he strode to the lectern and waited while the men opened the scrolls to his portion.

Trout now warmed up to the ceremony, chuckling at Ezra ben Gabirol's fervid anxiety which caused his hands to shake and top hat to bobble as he turned to remove the bindings of the Torah. He remembered Ezra describing the painstaking effort required to get a boy ready for this event: two years during which the boy is led to a consideration of the duties and excitements of his manhood. Ezra ben Gabirol spent as much of himself in the process as he extracted, a generosity which today was notably evident in the lad's elocution.

The boy was singing beautifully now. He traced the words on the parchment with a small pointer, lifting his face up from time to time to see if the audience was still with him. Although Harry Trout's knowledge of Hebrew was scant, he knew he was hearing the Story of Gideon. The tale of that extraordinary "ordinary" man seemed, to Harry Trout at any rate, particularly fitting for the occasion. He'd just gotten absorbed in the account of the battle with the Midianites when the lad stopped. At once a great relaxation rippled through the audience: the lad had come through in fine fashion. When he walked back to the arc to return the scroll, he had a definite spring to his stride.

From that point the service moved to its conclusion in a businesslike fashion. Ezra boomed the prayers, the lad answering with newly acquired authority, and the congregation chorused over all at a frightening pace. The cantor, whose solemnity had cast an awkward foreboding on the early proceedings, was now oversung by the others at the lectern. He seemed not a little resentful at this exclusion but no one seemed to care, the lure of the elaborate luncheon spread out and waiting in the vestry rooms below seemed now to be uppermost in everyone's mind. Trout noted that even the three patriarchs sharing the bench with him had awakened from their previous dour solemnity and were now skimming through the chants in a race to be done.

Then it was finished. Ezra led the lad off the pulpit and walked arm-in-arm with him down the aisle, nodding greetings. Upstairs the women were chattering and weeping; the men fumbled words of salutation to each other, anxious to get out of the rigid space between the benches. Then all filed out after the rabbi in a slow processional to join the women in the hallway outside.

Harry Trout fell in with this line which was queued up again to greet and congratulate the lad who stood shaking hands at the head of the vestry. Long, white-clothed tables had been set up against each wall on which was spread rows of silver and china platters embellished by glistening arrangements of special meat cuts, herring in wine sauce, sweet cakes and polished fruits.

The guests were very attentive to the boy, the women hugged and kissed him, the men shook his hand long enough to slip a bank note or two into it. He showed little surprise at this method of gift-giving, slipping the bills into his free hand, and holding his hand out anew for the next in line with considerable poise.

Most of the crowd was already seated at the tables

when Harry reached the Bar Mitzvah boy. He decided to bend with the custom, sliding a one pound note into the boy's hand as he paid respects.

"You did fine, young man!"

"Thank you, sir. I'm sorry, I don't know your name."

"Meet Detective Inspector Harry Trout, Clement. Mr. Trout is with the Metropolitan Police. And, Harry, I'd like you to meet Clement Davidovici, who today has added his strong voice to this congregation." Ben Gabirol glossed the amenities.

"Mr. Trout is an old friend, Clement. I knew him at school." He shook Trout's hand and put an arm on his shoulder. "What brings you to us today, Harry?"

"Business, Ezra, although I must say that up to now it's been all pleasure."

"Won't you have some sandwiches and cakes, Mr. Trout? I'll join you as soon as this line's over," Clement piped.

Trout smiled at the boy's politeness.

"Just a glass of punch, Clement, then I really must get back. Do you think you can spare the rabbi here for a few minutes?"

The lad's eyes widened. "It sounds like you're on a case, Inspector. Will you tell me about it?"

"When it's all over. Now I'm going to try that punch." He shook hands again with Clement, then made his way through the crowd about the punch bowl. Ezra joined him while he waited for a very fat lady with vivid rouged cheeks to ladle the red bubbly mixture into a crystal cup. He handed this to Ezra, took a second from her puffy fingers and moved to the edge of the crowd.

"Ezra, if it is convenient, I'd like to speak with you in your study. Will they mind if you leave?"

"No, of course not. The tension is over now. Everyone is relaxing."

They passed through the vestry and up a small flight of stairs to Ben Gabirol's tiny study. On the way up, Trout skimmed over some of his recent work, preferring not to talk directly about the case. When they reached the study he at on a rough wooden chair waiting for Ben Gabirol to get settled at his desk. Instead, the rabbi paced about the meager floor space, waiting for Trout to finish. Finally he cut the inspector off.

"Harry, you didn't come out to the synagogue this morning on your day off, wait patiently through the venerated Bar Mitzvah ceremony, even though I might say it was done in Bristol fashion, just to bring me up to date on your brilliant, if albeit a bit stormy career? Now what do you want to tell me?"

Trout, whose upbringing had been appropriately "old-fashioned," retained a solemn regard for clerics. Had he not known Ezra ben Gabirol better he would have been surprised, even shocked, by his matter-of-factness. He blushed now, not at the rabbi's candor, but rather at his own needless wordiness.

"As always, Ezra, you get right to the point." He flipped the amulet at the rabbi. "Without getting into its background, tell me what you can about this little trinket."

"That's a Sam, the Hebrew symbol for blood." He stopped pacing now and rolled the brass letter over in his hand. "It's part of the G'tach."

"The what?"

"The G'tach, the ten curses visited upon Pharaoh before the Exodus. Here, I'll show you."

He stepped to the side wall which was lined from floor to ceiling with books of every size and shape. He searched for a moment, then pulled a heavy leather-tooled volume from the next-to-bottom shelf, and placed it on a pedestal.

"As you know, the Jewish people lived for many generations in Egypt where they were treated with more or less hospitality, depending on the whim of the man on the throne and the practical politics of the times. During the time of Ramses II their condition worsened considerably, probably because of his construction project at Abu Simbel."

"They were pressed into slave labor?"

"Precisely. Health and safety precautions were rudimentary at best. The Egyptians, being a funerary people, had little regard for the amenities amongst their slaves. Work crews were driven relentlessly to meet construction deadlines. In the summer heat the toll, especially on the children and older people, was very great indeed. Jews have since recounted this suffering each year during the Passover which also celebrates their release from Egypt under Moses' leadership. To remind subsequent generations of the bitterness of their bondage, the Haggadah which is the literature of Passover, goes into quite a bit of descriptive detail and devotes some especially vivid language to the

G'tach."

"The G'tach is rather old, then?"

"If my calculations are correct, some 3,200 years. The G'tach is no more, no less than the essence of maledictions, solemn curses, anathemas wished against the Pharoahs for keeping the Israelites in bondage."

Trout scanned the trim heavy columns of Hebrew as the rabbi flipped the thick vellum pages. Finally he located a plate of ten engravings, each one illustrating an individual plague. He traced each scene as he enumerated: "Such things as the curse of blood, the curse of locusts, death of the first born, the curse of bats." His finger rested on this last.

Trout looked at the plate closely. Two dozen persons, dressed in the costumes of the day, were depicted. They'd been attacked by a swarm of black bats and now thrashed about in futile defense. Some had already fallen, and it is evident from the tears and scratches on their bodies that the others will soon drop under the animals' claws and sharp teeth. Trout looked quizzically at the rabbi. "Just a legend, of course?"

Ben Gabirol shook his head: "Oh, I think not!"

"Well, what I mean is, there have been all sorts of curses down through the ages— religious, mystical, the whole foundation of human retribution."

The rabbi was firm. "On the contrary, Harry, there's little doubt that the plagues did, in fact, occur, although so distant now as to *seem* almost a myth."

Trout pondered a bit. "These ten curses, did they follow any particular order?"

"That point has been debated by Talmudic scholars through the centuries. Ben Eleazer lists no order of preference. On the other hand, the great Akiba appears to have established a tradition by describing a sequence in which the curse of boils comes first, then frogs, bats, followed by the curse of blood, of rats, then of beasts, of locusts, and hail. The final curses are a bit difficult to contemplate: death of the first born—and darkness."

Trout was moved by this last: "Darkness, rabbi?"

Ben Gabirol was now fully caught up in the dream of the G'tach. His voice quivered with solemnity. "That ultimate curse was meant to bring a final onus upon the land. Dissolution, chaos, the whole nexus of the human contradiction. Night into day. And day into night. To forever end the sleep of man."

Trout was silent for a moment at Ben Gabirol's words, then repeated them as if to grasp their full portent: "To forever end the sleep of man?"

The rabbi shut the heavy book in conclusion. "Yes, Harry, the hand of death and darkness upon the land. The last and final curse of the G'tach."

The hand of death—darkness upon the land—fitting expletives for the rank atmosphere that swept the halls and staircases of the five-story brownstone on Maldine Square where the puppet orchestra sat stark and polished in the darkened ballroom. A vent of torpor seeped and eddied past the angular rigid portraiture of the family, ranked and rankling on the velvet-papered walls. A sullen blast of wind pressed through the wooden coping on the high ceiling trim. A death gush caught, clasped, choked off candles that lit hallways wanting darkness. A bitter ozone whipped and generated the dust along the carpet seams. A sinister zephyr banged against the curtains giving them the formful billows that whispered as ghosts in a lesser setting. A shade conjured Hamlet along a dozen windowpanes. A humor gave the grim hint to closed doors. A breeze blew black night into daytime chambers. Small jets of wind puffed fabric balls, a tornado surged from the floor posts in the basement.

Men slept by wind. A frosted face froze in wind. Intelligence wept the wind. Sails kept the wind. Mourners shuddered and crept in wind.

The mind was wind on death. Heresy got its start on wind. Buildings came apart in wind. Plots were laid in wind, conclusions made in wind, memories lost in wind.

The master of the letter "P"—how else could he be known—moved down the great interior staircase of the house on Maldine Square. His heels cut and clicked the air as he descended the ebony stairs; his coattails snapped the fragmented air behind. He had come from some chamber in the upper apartments and moved with uniform rapidity to reach a destination below. From his walk he appeared purposive, direct, although his features could not be seen clearly, shielded as they were by the white balustrade which snaked the length of the staircase.

This—white columns and railings edging polished ebony stairs—dominated the cavity of the building, soaring in an unwound oval from ground floor to ceiling 70 feet above. A pale moonlight filtered through glass panes in a petal pattern. From the center of these a heavy brass chandelier dropped down three floors branching into a multiple-globed lamp which was seldom turned on. Instead the staircase was lit at night, as it was this evening, by candle-lanterns hung at intervals along its length. His shadow rose and fell as he passed each lantern, flickering into a hundred variations along the cylindrical walls.

His footsteps continued their cadence. Now he passed along the third landing. Doors led off the hallway into its farthest reaches. A few steps and he was on the stairs again passing a pair of busts that occupied two niches along its inner wall. He gained the second landing, walking a bit slower now as he passed the massed portraiture of his family.

The resemblance was unmistakable. The cut of his clothes bore the same unswerving sobriety, his stance was equally rigid and unyielding, his head was held with the same perception, the same acute awareness. Yet he differed from his forebears: although his dress and surroundings marked him as a figure of the past, he alone was steeped in tragic dignity, in unbounded suffering.

He descended the final flight, his heels resounding closer now on the marble floor. He passed the large double doors to the ballroom and walked slowly, deliberately toward a room midway from the main hallway. He paused, inconsolably, as he reached the doorway, and then entered.

The room's interior exuded a rose glow. It appeared to

be a kind of shrine. Indeed, a full portrait of a young woman, finely featured and exquisite in every detail, was attached to one wall. This portrait was different from the others in the outer hall in that the subject's dress was contemporary and she wore her hair in the loose, fashionable style of the times. She could be his wife or his fiancée.

He fell to his knees at a small rosewood table placed beneath her picture. Then, moaning with unbelievable sadness, he lifted his eyes toward her. He rested at her shrine for a few moments, the pink lit lanterns softening somewhat his stark grief.

Then he rose and moved to an ornate wooden console which held an assortment of phonograph and radio equipment. Still glancing at the portrait he unfurled a long phono-jack from the console and plugged it into a receptacle in his neck. His eyes, withering in despair, darted back and forth from the portrait to the console. He moved a switch on the console.

One cannot have been ready for what followed. The timbre of his voice and the compressed violence of his delivery were edged in a hardness out of all proportion to the grief he bore. Now he spoke for the first time, harsh, metallic, rattling and thoroughly ominous, filling the room with a terror that was at once unnatural and unwonted.

"My love, sweet queen and noble wife, I alone remain to bring delivery of your pain, severed, my darling, too quickly, from this life. Of tears drawn and memories met, I shall hold our two hearts again in single time."

His voice continued to bang from the console's speaker, drawing a chilled, detached texture from its mechanical source.

"Nine killed you, nine shall die and be returned your loss. Nine times nine. Nine killed you. Nine shall die. Nine eternities in doom."

He tapered off, apparently wasted from the exertion.

"Nine killed you, nine shall die. Darkness. The tenth. To move the earth its final sleep." Now near the end of his strength he pulled the plug from his neck, and threw it back onto the console. Slowly, and with obvious exertion, he advanced toward the far end of the room.

This contained dressers, side tables, glass cases and other dressing room furniture done in walnut about which was arranged his wife's gowns, scarves, wrappers and other personal belongings. That she was a young woman when she died was attested to by the verve and style of her wardrobe: a white tennis outfit edged in blue and red stripes, a purple ballgown sewn with silver sequins, black lace gloves with matching black lace shoes, a fantastic green satin coat cinched by a silver belt, a leopard muff.

He opened the drawers slowly, wearily, drawing out a dress here, a scarf there, to admire it, folding and replacing it with great sadness afterwards. The shelving bore her cosmetics, some perfume bottles and a collection of needlepoint. A group of dolls filled another cabinet.

He moved about her possessions stiffly. Their nearness only seemed to have submerged his grief rather than deadened it. His gloved hands touched the furniture and traced a futile pattern from piece to piece. Against all their varied colors, against the vivacity of his young dead wife, he seemed to grow even more forlorn. Finally, he moved toward the front of the room, glanced once more at his wife's picture, and left. Tears were streaming down his face now.

One can only approximate the perception of this ravaged, forlorn man as he lost himself again in the reaches of this strange domain on Maldine Square. A man of obvious intelligence and deep personal resource, he seems as much mechanical as made of flesh and blood. His total human landscape was polarized by an unyielding grief and equally rigid hatred. He lived, but one wondered why! He hoped — but for what? His days were an accumulation of grievous dreams of deliverance — when? His plans, intricate and of an inspired genius — were for what?

Chapter 8

HARRY Trout liked to stay in bed late Sunday mornings, eating peeled oranges and reading the *Times*, which he had delivered to his door. Even when he was at school in the midst of examinations, he wouldn't allow the press of work to interrupt this ritual. And although he kept his grades up, it was bandied about that young Trout was a bit of a cutup—a bon vivant rather than a scholar. The reputation had stuck with him.

This particular Sunday came at the end of a week's worth of fine weather, and was appropriately murky. The fog settled in the night before and now it was raining, hard enough in fact to keep up a steady drumroll on the copper-shingled roof above.

The *Times* news section had been mercifully brief, the less than three pages devoted to the interminable disarmament conferences, warship tonnage ratios seeming to be the main topic of those conversations. The delegates to the League of Nations meeting in Lausanne, affirming their position *against* hunger, had decided to organize a committee to study it and subsequently to form a commission to deal with the scourge.

Properly obscure on page 3 was an in-depth report of the inflationary spiral now taking place in Germany. The writer seemed anxious to conclude that this nation, which had gone down in ignominious military defeat less than a decade earlier, was now about to sustain an equally devastating economic defeat. "Philosophical excesses were at fault," concluded the reporter; he neglected any mention of the new politics then in process in Central Europe.

Trout was pleased, if a bit miffed, to find no word of the doctors' murders. Although he was too professional to dwell overlong on it, the official rebuke he'd received for his "aggressiveness" was fresh enough in his thoughts that he wanted no repetition. He also realized that his plans for advancement within the department required a self-imposed obscurity for the time being. He was properly glad, therefore, that the case, already a week old, had managed to stay out of the papers. Nevertheless, like all men of self-assured brilliance, he was a performer at heart and would have been happier in the limelight.

But it was Sunday and no time for scruffy concerns such as these. He glanced at his watch and was surprised to find the time had gotten well past three with the sports and library section yet to be read. All that would have to wait. He was hungry now, which thought reminded him it'd been too late yesterday for him to shop before he came home.

He tried to recall what the kitchen had in store while he fumbled for his slippers under the bed. There was a loaf of pumpernickel in the bread box: probably crusty, but still edible. That would go good with those sausages in the refrigerator. He'd gotten a crock of mustard the week before so there was still some left. A bottle or two of port to wash it down would make it lunch enough.

He found his shoes and was just tying shut his dressing gown when the telephone rang. The voice was direct, discursive.

"Inspector Trout? Vesalius here. Can you get over in thirty minutes. I will want to discuss some matters with you."

So the ramrod was beginning to bend. Well, let's set the book first, Trout thought. "Dr. Vesalius, good of you to call. Can what you have keep till tomorrow? It's Sunday, you know, a day of rest. Why don't I stop by on my way to the office in the morning?"

Vesalius was firm. "That won't do, Mr. Trout. I'm leaving for Durham tomorrow for a few days. It'll have to be this afternoon."

"If you insist. Can we make it in one hour? I haven't had lunch."

"Forty-five minutes. And please be prompt." The receiver clicked off.

"Once a bastard, always a bastard," Harry whistled through his teeth as he kicked off his slippers and reached for a pair of socks.

Ten minutes later he was racing out the door, raincoat and umbrella tucked under one arm, working briefcase in the other. The sausage and port would have to wait. Whatever it was Vesalius had to say he didn't think he'd called him out to discuss the weather.

When Trout got there he wasn't disappointed. He was ushered in by a young boy aged fourteen or fifteen, whose marked resemblance to his father stamped him with the same reserve, the same driving precision as the older Vesalius. Nevertheless, he was pleasant enough, taking Trout's now-soaked raincoat while he showed him into the apartment.

"Hello. You're Inspector Trout. My father is expecting you, please come this way." His handshake had a genuine if unexpected warmth.

Trout looked about, half expecting the senior Vesalius to be squatting amongst his trains. But he was nowhere in sight.

"Trout—in here," a voice called.

He followed the sound of the voice, walking past the trains and down a single stair into the study beyond.

Vesalius stood opposite, behind a large slab table on which stacks of officious manila folders indicated that he'd indeed been busy. He stood up as Trout entered, looked at him blandly, anchored his fingers together and began speaking in his characteristically dry manner.

"At your last visit, Inspector, I must confess a preoccupation with other matters, and perhaps, did not give you as much attention as you may have felt requisite. Of course, we needn't belabor the footnote to these . . . cases, as you call them—that doctors are as likely to die strange deaths as anyone else, perhaps more likely than most. A schoolday friend, and one of the most popular punters our class had, passed away under bizarre circumstances. He contrived to get bitten by one of the experimental animals in a tropical medicine class. Suffice it to say that the animal was a mamba.

"At first your observations, as you referred to them, simply didn't jell together enough to make a 'case' even though the temptation was at hand. I hadn't seen Thornton for about three years, and differing schedules kept me from seeing much of Dunwoody and Hargreaves. It was quite comfortable to believe at the time you made your presentation, that these men had, somehow, all become fanciers of pets. Not so far-fetched when you consider the mess the average dog can create."

Trout, who'd been reclining in a large, leather, swayback chair during Vesalius' excursion, was moved to comment by this last vaguery: "I'm sure that even a man of such catholic tastes as yours, Doctor, would be hard pressed to discover the endearing qualities of bats, let alone to keep them loose in great quantities in an apartment"

Vesalius was unphazed. "For the record, Inspector, animals of all kinds repell me, which fact certainly doesn't prevent others from exercising their whims. But pets and their masters are not what concerns us here today."

"I think not," Trout agreed.

"My doubt—reservation would be more descriptive— dissolved at poor Longstreet's death. I greatly respected his dedication, and saw him rather regularly at the clinicopathological conferences he organized in the charity wards. His economy kept him apart from the usual round of meetings, luncheons and conferences that afflict the average doctor. He was as poor as a vicar. This meant little to him; he gave his best to that dingy little examination room in Chelsea, serving persons less fortunate. Wesley Longstreet was a man to be admired. His loss will hurt the profession. It certainly has troubled me."

Trout nodded, not wanting to disturb him.

"When I called at your office I told you I was into something which would occupy me for a few days." He gestured at the manila folders. "These are case files. When you hear what I've got to say, I think you will understand why I have called you here."

Trout urged him on: "Shoot!"

Vesalius coughed to clear his throat. "Very well then. Three years ago I retired from my surgical practice for personal reasons, which seemed compelling enough at the time. Since then I've limited myself to consultation with an occasional direct participation in a case. The book which I'd set out to do remains unfinished."

"We all get bitten at least once." Trout hardly concealed his amusement at finding a weakness in this otherwise rigid man.

Vesalius ignored him. "Toward that, I've kept a record of every case I've served on in the last decade; some twelve hundred in all." He removed a short stubby German-made cigar from a humidor, lighted it amidst luxurious blue puffs, and resumed, punching the air with his cigar for effect. "As you know, modern surgery is all teamwork, often requiring as many as a dozen people: surgeons, anesthetists, internists, as well as other specialists." He shuffled through the folders, talking as he scanned their labels: "If we rule out all cases older than five years, the year that poor Dunwoody, our "bat victim" resumed practice in London, there was a total of thirty-seven cases in which I served with any two of the four deceased men. Thirty-seven out of twelve hundred. The cases in which any three of us served is reduced to a scant dozen." He puffed and watched Trout to register his reaction. "And there was only one case —just one—where all of us worked together."

He extracted a single folder, handed it across the table to Trout who stood opposite Vesalius now.

Trout read aloud while he thumbed through the folder: "Victoria Regina Phibes. Born November 27, 1893 . . . married . . . no children . . . diagnosis: metastatic carcinoma of the uterus." Trout looked up. "That's a rough shake."

Vesalius nodded. "As rough as they come," he said.

Trout continued. "Recommendation: immediate radical resection." He turned the page and stopped at the hospital admissions sheet which contained Victoria Phibes' snapshot. He studied this for a moment, then closed the cover and looked squarely at Vesalius. "She's very beautiful. What happened?"

"The operation was routine, if you can call ten hours of dissection, routine. But as is the rule in cases like this, good surgery is seldom enough. There were complications; she died in the recovery room."

Trout was not moved. "Did you know her personally, Doctor?"

Vesalius took the folder from Trout and placed it back in the stack. "Yes, and no. She was a comparatively new patient. I'd seen her a few times at the hospital—casually, not professionally. Then, of course, she was admitted and we operated almost at once."

Trout looked at the folder which Vesalius had placed atop one stack. "She would be difficult to forget."

"Quite a beautiful young woman. Even in death there was a strange presence about her. I remember being puzzled that she had no visitors while she was in the recovery room."

Trout started. "What about the husband?"

"He was in Switzerland at the time. A Dr. Anton Phibes. We cabled him of course . . ."

"And?"

Vesalius looked off. "You know, tragedy has a way of doubling itself. The car he was driving went off the road in the Juras. He was burned to death in the crash."

Trout looked up sharply. "You're sure about that, Doctor?"

Vesalius sat back in his seat and spoke with minor triumph. "It must seem a tempting theory for you, Inspector, but I recall reading reports of the funeral. Both the husband and his lady were interred at the same time in the family vault outside of London."

Trout began to pace, talking with the beat of his walk. "Together in eternal repose; they must've been quite fond of each other."

Vesalius nodded in agreement. "Like Troilus and Cressida, Abelard and Heloise. It would seem that they were completely devoted."

Trout stopped pacing and, gazing at Vesalius, spoke now in an even tone: "We've also set the entire surgical teams' death sentence. Someone, for whatever reason, has damned them everybody listed here—to eternal retribution. And that includes you." His face darkened. "Had we known about this yesterday, we might've been able to save Longstreet's life."

Vesalius was shaken. "Don't you think I've already thought of that? Common decency would have demanded that I speak out. Please know that it matters to me little what you think, Inspector. But I will vouchsafe the fact that this connection we've described here was unknown to me as late as today's breakfast."

"I didn't mean to imply that you'd been remiss, Doctor."

"On the contrary, you were merely stipulating a causality. But enough of this ratiocination. It is to be hoped that the remaining persons involved—that would be Drs. Hedgepeth, Kitaj, Whitcomb and who else— he fumbled— "That's it, Nurse Allan."

Trout interrupted amiably. "You're forgetting the ninth victim, Doctor." Vesalius was puzzled. Trout broke the spell: "Yourself, Doctor Vesalius. You served on that team."

"Yes, but only as a consultant. I don't know if I am qualified for the—for the execution. However, I do have a further question for you, Inspector. Eight or nine persons served on that surgical floor. What are your plans to protect the remaining survivors? Although heaven knows from what."

Trout brought it to a point, his voice low and solid. "The G'tach."

Vesalius picked it right up. "The curse of the pharaohs?"

Trout prepared to leave. He walked forward to the other room and the far doorway with Vesalius at his elbow. Both men had come face to face with the stark dimension of the case, realizing at once that someone or something was bringing murder into their lives for reasons which were definitely, damnably obscure. The afternoon's conversation had brought that realization and its chastening effects to them.

Trout accepted his raincoat and umbrella from Vesalius' son, and thanking him, waited for the boy to leave before he had a last word with the doctor.

"It seems clear, Doctor, that someone is using the ancient biblical curses of the G'tach to kill all those involved in Victoria Phibes' operation. It is a grim, ironic, deadly response but, nevertheless, one which must be reckoned with."

Vesalius replied in a near whisper. "But *who*, Inspector?"

Trout opened the door. "The husband's dead. There are no children. The tragedies happened years ago. I'll ask *you*, Doctor—who the hell are we looking for?"

The rain had stopped when Harry Trout reached the pavement and a few stars had broken through the high, patchy clouds. The air had a clean, washed smell made more fragrant by the still damp buds on the young trees. A few rain puddles glistened on the sidewalk and there was very little traffic. A good spring night.

But Harry Trout wasn't very interested in spring nights nor clean air. He disliked having his day off ruined and now he was mulling over a case that'd seemed headed in the right direction when he laid it out with Schenley over Scotch and sodas the day before. Now Vesalius had changed all that by shifting from the disdainful professional to the dedicated amateur. But the man's induction had been unassailable. It had to be acknowledged. If only his logic hadn't led to a blind alley.

He stepped off the curb and right into a water puddle. Cursing now, he hurried across the street and jumped into his car. Rather than fight the saucepans at home, he'd grab a beef sandwich somewhere and go right to bed when he got home. Tomorrow was Monday.

Men had different ways to launch the week than those fortunate enough to be self-accountable for their time. Some made checklists, others reviewed files or plotted on blackboards, still others drank large amounts of coffee, orange juice or whatever they could to counteract the night before. For Harry Trout, a half-hour on the handball court set him right for whatever else that came along the rest of the day.

To a very few men, and these were either very rich or unemployed, Monday was just one day in the week. These men took in stride this singular day, the week's inaugural, whose tyranny had enslaved the bulk of the wage-earning population in dulled acceptance and disbelief for generations. These very few men met Mondays on equal terms while most of their colleagues hated or feared this week's first day.

Dr. Arthur Hedgepeth belonged to this former group. Born rich and marrying into even greater wealth, Arthur Hedgepeth condescended to enter the profession late in his life, not out of any dedication, but rather of a fear of prolonged ennui. He surprised everyone but himself by gaining entry to the University of Edinburgh's highly regarded medical school, where he conducted himself in exemplary fashion and graduated with honors. These were awarded grudgingly, and there was no doubt in his and his instructors' minds that they came as a result of his meritorious performance and for no other Eason. Academicians waste little affection on the scions of the very wealthy.

But the Hedgepeth fortune, if it hindered his acceptance in all but a few circles during his scholastic career, afforded him the luxury of rejecting illusions in favor of practical judgments. He was to use this approach to his subsequent professional course with effect. Characteristically, Hedgepeth chose surgery when the time came to select an internship, because he recognized quite clearly that although innovation in medical research was beyond his reach, distinction in this most "solid" of the medical arts was not. Throughout his long career which had already spanned five decades, Arthur Hedgepeth was to demonstrate the correctness of this choice time and time again.

In the early years he worked diligently, putting in far more hours than he planned. He took routine cases as well as some not routine, gaining in the course of his practice the honor of his patients and the acknowledgment of his colleagues. He was "a man who knew his business." This state of affairs suited him fine, fitting in rather well with his own self-assessment that he was a "journeyman surgeon." When he reached sixty, he permitted himself the one extravagance that comes with age and commensurate wealth. He worked only when he cared to.

On Mondays, Dr. Hedgepeth did not care to work. Rather, he enjoyed motoring, which he did whenever the weather permitted. For that purpose he purchased a Bentley sedan and had it furnished with all the comforts of a touring car. He would give orders to his chauffeur to bring the car around at six, at which precise time he would embark on an all-day excursion to the Lake District, to Cornwall, to Devon or some other place that caught his fancy. On days when the weather held he would take lunch from a wicker hamper prepared the night before, turning back for home after a two-hour repast at a roadside park.

On this, the second Monday in May, he was en route to Pevensey to visit the site where Duke William first set foot in England with his Norman followers. Benson, his chauffeur of thirty years, was driving up front, his eyes quite intent on the road because of the fog. They had already passed through the London environs and were now negotiating the park like greenbelt south of the city. It was not quite seven and few cars were on the road.

Hedgepeth sat in the rear, bundled against the fog's chill, smoking his breakfast cigar. He looked at the scenery with little interest since the fog was still rather thick.

Suddenly something on the road up ahead caught his attention.

"Pull over, Benson," he said, tapping on the chauffeur's window.

A long saloon car was stopped in distress at the side of the pavement. Hedgepeth was distracted by the sight of the young lady who stood, helpless and forlorn, next to the car's open cowl. "Stop here, Benson, and see what you can do."

Benson glided the Bentley to a stop some twenty feet behind the saloon car. He turned to his master to confirm his wishes. "Shall I get out, sir?"

Hedgepeth was by now quite absorbed by the car up ahead. The fog lay low on the ground and they seemed to be out in the middle of a deserted field. He could not determine the make of the car, certainly not its difficulty. He cared little about that anyway, preferring to look much more closely at the narrow waist and fine ankles of the young woman who still bent over the motor. He barely acknowledged his chauffeur, only wishing he would get out there and possibly manage an introduction. When the man seemed to hesitate, he hurried him on his way. "Yes, yes, of course, Benson, see what the lady needs."

Benson slid out, closing the door with a soft "chug" and walked forward to the car, his steps muffled by the fog. Hedgepeth resumed his scrutiny of the girl. She seemed to be wearing a heavy, black, fur-trimmed greatcoat which was cut rather high on her legs over tall black leather boots; these were laced up to her calf. She balanced on one foot, extending her other leg out behind as she delved into the mystery of the car's motor. Her soft white knees and lower thighs were softened further by the fog and seemed to glow against the polished black surface of the saloon car. Periodically, her bell-shaped rump bobbed as she dug further into the cowl. He sighed at this vision and waited impatiently for Benson to reach the car.

Now she moved a bit, her rump sliding enticingly along the chrome plate with the motion of her legs. Even more thigh became visible. Hedgepeth craned his neck and leaned forward. "Aha! Benson is introducing himself!"

At that, the rear door opposite to the one at which he peered clicked open. The draft disturbed Hedgepeth long enough for him to do two things. First, he glanced over at the door in time to stare directly into the blazing eyes of a man he'd never seen before. And, concomitantly, he shifted his glance in sheer self-defense to the closest object moving within his field of vision.

That object was a metronome, now ticking. It would continue to tick through and past the final minutes of his life.

Chapter 9

IN contrast to the stillness of that fog-bound fen, it was an unquiet Monday in the house on Maldine Square. On the lower floors the dusk of the long night slowly gave over to the filtering daylight, the house creaking and groaning as if trying to reconstitute itself for the new week.

The ballroom had apparently been the scene for a gala the previous evening. A large canvas backdrop, depicting the Casino Royale in its most lavish transports, had been pulled down over one wall. In front of the massed revelers and milling waiters, who looked slightly out of place in the morning light in the ballroom, the solitary café table, its glassed rose beginning to wilt, seemed forlorn indeed. The ballroom had the inescapable look of all nightclubs in the first morning hours: it was unhappy. Even the musicians' too-white teeth framed in their smiles, pencil-thin mustaches and slick hair worn by the gigolos of the day, seemed weary.

The day had come more quickly to the top floor, where much hissing and shuffling about indicated that the Master of the Letter "P" found much to busy himself with this

Monday.

The entire fifth floor, which was the uppermost one in the building, had been given over completely to a combination observatory/laboratory, a very large room, some 125' by 30', which looked more like a loft than an apartment. It abounded with windows, these being interspersed with slanted, paneled walls. The fifth floor itself, which towered 15' above the adjacent buildings, actually formed the base of the roof. Its exterior walls were not flat but sloped sharply upward a dozen feet where they joined the roof proper. Viewed from the front, the whole superstructure had the appearance of a raised hexagon, its top peaked by a lightning rod. The roof, angled sides as well as flatter top, was clad with copper, its blue oxidized surface contrasting with the somber cut slate exterior finish of the floors below. Like its neighbors, the building was a stately, formal residence in full command of a decorum befitting the occupants of Maldine Square.

The fifth floor observatory had a 360 degree view of London. A large land telescope had been mounted at one window. In another, which had been fitted with a retractable skylight, a refractory telescope was installed for celestial viewing. This instrument, polished brass driven by a stainless steel gear mechanism, appeared to be custom-designed for maximum precision. A stellar map of the heavens and charts of the stars' proper motions hung on the wall near the refractor.

A long bench directly to the rear contained a full-scale analytical chemical laboratory. A distillation apparatus, precision balance, drying oven and centrifuge crowded its surface amongst Bunsen burners, flasks and beakers of all sizes and racks of test tubes. Suspended the length of the bench on uprights were double rows of three-tiered shelving, crowded with blown-glass jars and bottles of purified reagents. At the very center of the room a Foucault pendulum suspended by a steel wire rope inexorably tolled the motion of the earth. To the left of this stood a life-size figure of a man. The figure was constructed of intricately interwoven skin layers, organs and bones, each of a naturally colored hardened rubber composition, cut in cross-section to illustrate the anatomic details. More remarkably, the figure could be cleaved at other layers and angles to show different structures.

The room seemed to spread in all directions, offering an infinite variety of complex devices, precision measuring instruments, physical charts, and blackboards crammed with equations of great summary. In its total prospect the observatory could be likened to the study of a Renaissance scholar who, at the infancy of scientific knowledge, had an interest in all of its parts.

But the scholar of this elaborate room had somewhat more specific interests this Monday morning as he lumbered about a black-cloth shielded portion of his laboratory. He wore a long white laboratory smock and a white gauze hat on his head and looked every bit the occult medicine man as he hovered over a circle of waxen life masks arranged on a rough bench. Hissing sounds came from the orifice in his neck as he fondled and genuflected over the masks. He seemed to be seeking out one in particular. Then he found it, his eyes flashing, his laughter boiling over into scalding peals, he grabbed it from the table, holding the prize up in the sanguinary triumph of an executioner. The face was no other than that of Dr. Arthur Hedgepeth, suspended now with great finitude in the rubber-gloved hands of this wizard. He hissed again, scalding the air once more in compressed fury. Then, slamming the effigy back down on the table, he grabbed a squat, mean-looking blowtorch, and igniting it with a spark, proceeded to melt away Hedgepeth's features which slid, and finally sank, in waxen agony. Soon, the blowtorch had reduced Hedgepeth's face to a featureless shell, its core now a lumped residue at the base of the head. Glistening out from the center of the still bubbling wax was another brass amulet; a "charad," the Hebrew symbol for hail.

Big Ben was tolling 9 A.M. and the streets were crowded with the last-dash latecomers racing to beat the morning starting bell. Monday was a day definitely to be early but it seemed that on this day there were more late travelers than usual.

Harry Trout, who'd grown resigned to the exigencies of traffic, was amongst these unfortunates. And, out of their sheer mathematical overbearing, rather than from any specific commission on his part, he reached his office ten minutes later than usual. He debated briefly at the elevator bank whether to have his usual handball match, and was surprisingly relieved when the "up" car arrived first. It was to be the office.

Tom Schenley was waiting for him. His bland expression told Trout that nothing untoward had occurred so far that day, for which he was thankful. Tom had also readied two cups of coffee which now rested, steaming and inviting, on his desk. For these he was doubly thankful. He threw his hat on a corner hatrack, grabbed a cup, and sat back in his tilt-back chair waiting for Schenley to speak.

The sergeant began with his usual forthrightness. "Harry—" he only called him Harry when he was reaching for something "profound"—"You and I have been in this business long enough to know that the initiative must pass to us sooner or later."

"That's a rather gloomy beginning for you this morning, Tom. Had a bad weekend, did you?"

"No sir. It's this bloody case. I hate to say it but it's had me thinking all week. I even got in a fight with my wife; said I took my office home with me, she did."

Trout chided him, "Nan wouldn't say something like that unless she had good reason. You should have kissed her on the cheek and taken her out to a good show."

"We started to, but it was raining too hard. Played cribbage instead and drank toddies. Those damned animals stayed with me the whole time."

His partner's constraint sobered Trout. "Of course you're right, Tom, police officers are always playing ball with the other side. The law tells us that we have to build a case. Our honorable opponents are not, of course, bound by such prosaic considerations. And so they are forced to act in their own best self-interest, which is, by definition, outside the law." He sipped his coffee. "Good detection is simply efficient second-guessing."

"Well, I'd like to start guessing right. It's a helluva note to sit back and let someone knock these blokes off."

Trout brightened up. "Maybe we can change the odds a bit. Our old friend Dr. Vesalius called me over to his place yesterday. Said he'd done some careful thinking and wanted to see me about it. When I got there, he'd pulled out a stack of records, going back ten years. We discussed a number of the men, some of whom were already familiar. One of them I want you to get a line on, a Dr. Anton Phibes."

Schenley cut him off by highlighting the known history of this man to Trout's growing astonishment. "British foreign servant and career diplomat . . . married a blue-blooded beauty, Victoria Regina Devereux, some fifteen years younger than him . . . known as a devoted couple . . . moved in literary and artistic circles. She died following surgery for advanced carcinoma of the uterus. Ironically he died the same day in a motor accident in Switzerland. Car left the road as he raced home to be at her side."

Trout leaned back in his swivel chair, his face broadening into a wide grin as his associate displayed his efforts. When Tom finished, the Inspector banged the desk with his palm. "Where the hell did you come up with that?"

Schenley was modest. "Vesalius called first thing this morning. Said something about not going north after all. Asked if we'd done anything with Phibes. I figured the name was important. Incidentally, his insurance and bank accounts were all closed by the Swiss concern that handled his estate."

"And his residence?"

"The same bank had the whole place—possessions, clothing, furniture, everything was auctioned off. Not a trace left. Nothing." The phone rang. Schenley looked at Trout, a flicker of hesitation on his face as if he were almost afraid to answer. "That's probably Vesalius again." He picked up the receiver.

Both men kept a thick silence on their way out to Dunton Green. News of a murder affects even the most seasoned police officers. News of Hedgepeth's death, coming in such close sequence after the others, was a particularly hard blow for both Trout and Schenley. Needless to say, as the men most closely associated with the case, they would have been expected to take some preventive steps. But the manpower shortage within the department, and the murderer's own accelerating timetable had stymied any workable plan of defense. Trout knew that that would have to change. And, like Schenley had expressed earlier, he now found himself acutely wishing for a shift of the initiative.

The road had been reasonably clear with the high overcast yielding to good visibility as they traveled through the North London areas of Lewisham and Bromley. But as their car left Orpington and started through the open fields and wooded hillsides of the greenbelt further north, a low ground fog developed which forced them to slow down to less than twenty miles per hour in some spots.

Trout was anxious to reach the murder site, and kept wiping the windshield with his handkerchief to better see the road ahead. Schenley kept the windshield wipers going against the fog droplets, their "squish-squash" adding to the motor's drone. They edged through the hamlet of Dunton Green, scarcely detecting it because of the fog, and began navigating the road to the south. This was a particularly desolate section surrounded by well-grazed fields out of which rose an occasional tree, its damp black branches and trunk ghostly in the fog.

"Up ahead, Tom, they're over to the side of the road." It was the first Trout had spoken the entire trip.

Schenley pulled their limousine directly behind the local police cars that were parked along the dirt shoulder of the road. A local sergeant waved to them as they got out. "Over here, Inspector. They found him sitting off to the side of the road."

The sergeant joined Trout as he crossed to the stopped police car. "I'm afraid he's quite out of it," the man continued in a low voice.

It was Benson, Hedgepeth's chauffeur. The locals had found him lying by the roadside. He was in such a bad way that they'd wrapped him in a blanket and propped him up in the back of one car until help could come. When Trout looked inside the car, the man was still sitting there like a mute vegetable, his eyes and mouth wide-open in a frozen expressionless gaze. Occasionally he would whine the low, hurt moan of an animal badly handled.

"What happened to him?" Trout queried the sergeant.

"We don't know. He's in a dangerous state of shock that had him damn near fibrillating. Whatever he's been through or seen has about frightened him to death," the sergeant replied sadly.

Trout shook his head, controlling his anger. "Where's Hedgepeth?"

The sergeant nodded to the Bentley which was somewhat apart from the other cars. Its low shape was partly obscured by the fog, out of which it rose like some black memorial. The car's cowl had been raised and its windows and doors, which were all closed tight, were frosted over.

"He's in the back." The sergeant pointed to the rear door as he and Trout walked along the dirt toward the car. Trout stepped directly to it, grabbed the door handle and pulled his hand away instantly. "Wow, that's cold!"

He put on his gloves and tried again, this time yanking the door open to emit a dense vaporous billow from inside the car. When it cleared he bent low and peered inside. There, seated like a king in mufti, was Arthur Hedgepeth, his gray bulk covered by hundreds of thousands of hailstones which filled the Bentley's rear compartment up to his armpits.

"That looks like number four," said Tom Schenley, who'd slipped up on the sergeant and Trout.

"I have little doubt about it." Trout gritted his teeth and reached into the rear of the car to pick out a handful of the hailstones. "The curse of hail in the bloody middle of nowhere."

He threw the hailstones away in anger. The sergeant opened the front door and pointed to a galvanized metal ice machine which rested on the front seat. A dull, sullen nozzle pointed through the open glass divider directly at Hedgepeth. Cables led through the crack on top of the doorway to the motor. The sergeant reached in and gingerly positioned the nozzle so that it pointed outside. "He worked it off the motor; brought the car's internal temperature down below zero when it was going full blast."

He started the machine, its nozzle emitting a blast of hail. "Mercifully he didn't feel much."

Trout was grim. "Like hell he didn't!" He walked back toward his limousine. Schenley noticed that his shoulders sagged slightly. It was near dusk and the fog was thicker. It would be a long, slow ride home in the darkness.

Later that night the weather turned cold, cold enough for Henri Vesalius to put an extra log on the fire. He'd been deep in a chess game with his son Lem, and hadn't noticed that the room had grown frigid. The log was a very dry liveoak round that burst into a sheet of crackling flames and sparks as soon as he dropped it into the embers of the two previous logs. He fixed himself a Scotch and soda while he was up and returned to the low table at which Lem, dressed in pajamas and robe, was in the act of moving his knight.

"Check," the boy said, cornering his king.

Vesalius, with two rooks and a bishop remaining on the board, still had a position strong enough to ward off this attack. But he had fallen deep into thought and was obviously not interested in the game.

"Check," Lem urged again.

Vesalius now looked at the board, sighed and sipped his drink. "I guess that's it, Lem. Now off to bed with you."

The boy didn't like to see his father this way. "It's not mate, Father, you can still move."

Vesalius had drifted back into thought again. "What? Oh . . . well, we can finish tomorrow. You played very well, son. Now, up you go."

Lem, sensing that his father was heavily absorbed, reluctantly got up to leave. As he passed the side table he picked up a piece of sheet music and nodded toward the piano. "Would you like to hear that Chopin sonata I just got?"

Vesalius declined. "No, not tonight. I'm rather bad company, I'm afraid. Go on up and read for a little. I'll be up in a bit."

"That's all right, Father, I understand. But you must let me play this piece for you tomorrow. Old Darrow put me onto it. It's super."

Vesalius looked puzzled. "Darrow?"

"You know, the old chap at the music shop where I go for my pieces. I used to think him such a bore, but he's got a great memory. Do you know that he can recall the dates when Beethoven first published his symphonies, the names of each of Bach's children, and thousands of other bits of information that you'd never think possible?"

"Sounds like a good man to know. Here, it's after eleven, and tomorrow's a school day. Good night, Lem."

"Good night, Father."

Henri Vesalius sat alone in his parlor for some time after his son went to bed. He drank his Scotch slowly and with great deliberation, periodically looking at the chessboard, the wall paintings, the sleek model trains. Finally he turned off the lights and went up to his bedroom.

Early the next morning Henri Vesalius paid a call on the proprietor of the X-pert Music Shoppe out on Romford Road. He'd checked the address in the telephone book at coffee and was reasonably certain that the Romford Road address matched Lem's general description. When he got to the place, he knew he'd guessed correctly when he saw that worthy's name imprinted in gold lettering on the front door glass: Benedict Darrow, Prop.

He went in to the accompaniment of a string of harness bells which had been tacked above the door to warn the proprietor of a customer's arrival. Apparently this system wasn't working on that particular morning as Vesalius, unmet at the door, penetrated the musty store unmolested.

Like most other music shops, Darrow's shelves were crammed with texts and cord-or-staple-bound sheet music. *The yellowed covers couldn't help but arouse the curiosity,* thought Vesalius as he scanned the packed rows. There was still no sign of Mr. Darrow or any customer for that matter, and Vesalius roamed at will. Finally, he found what he was looking for: a large loose-leaf folder tucked away on the next-to-the-top shelf. Its black leather edge bore no title but someone, probably a collector, had typed a piece of medical plaster on which the word "Playbills" was scrawled in thin hand.

Vesalius quickly rolled the traveling ladder into position and climbed up to retrieve the binder. He thumbed through it for a few moments while perched on the ladder, then, finding what he'd been seeking, called out to the still invisible proprietor.

"Mr. Darrow. Mr. Darrow, are you back there?"

Not even the floors creaked in the old shop. Vesalius clambered down, prize in hand, and went back toward the rear in search of the reticent Darrow.

He found him a few minutes later after searching some pitch black cubicles where, in better times, operatic singers had come to try out the new song publications.

Darrow had sequestered himself in one of these chambers. When Vesalius came upon him, that frail octogenarian was perched atop a tall stool; a pair of earphones bound about his head on top of which he wore a tall, embroidered skullcap. A Victrola was playing on a nearby desk and Darrow was listening rapturously, a beatific gaze affixed to his myopic face, to whatever it was that was playing.

Vesalius hated to disturb the gentleman, but the press of the business at hand compelled him to take overt action. He placed the binder on the desk next to the Victrola and tapped the old man gently on the shoulder. "Mr. Darrow!"

A minute or two passed, and when the proprietor finally opened his eyes, Vesalius was touched by the serene even vision of some personal destiny contained in their deep, if myopic firmament. Abruptly he pulled off the earphones, sending the crashing tonality of a symphony orchestra instantly from their open speakers. His spell broken, Darrow climbed off the stool, turned the Victrola down with resignation and faced his customer.

Vesalius continued. "Mr. Darrow, did you ever know this man?" He showed him a loose handbill that'd been included in the collection. It pictured a youngish, very handsome man, dressed in a tuxedo, seated at a large pipe organ, underneath which was printed the dates: March 20, 21, 22, and the place, Giffard's Theatre, in small black letters. At the bottom of the sheet the performer's name was printed in considerably larger letters that read: Anton Phibes.

Darrow squinted at the type, then screwed his face up toward Vesalius. "Giffard's Theatre. That old barn burned down fifteen years ago. Some darned soprano dropped a cigarette in her dressing room."

Vesalius was impatient. "Yes, of course, Mr. Darrow, but what about the performer? Did he ever buy any music here?"

Darrow put down the magnifying glass through which he'd been eyeing the handbill and began putting on the earphones again. He squinted at Vesalius a last time before retreating to his reverie and said: "He still does!"

Chapter 10

WHEN Henri Vesalius left the X-pert Music Shoppe, he had a slightly giddy feeling. He seemed taller, or at least the pavement rose in a different perspective. His walk was heavy, more resonant; his heels matched the curb in hardness. The late afternoon air was elegant, crisp, stiffening to his skin. Its pristine clarity gave the sun enormous volume; the large yellow disc plaqued to the air on a flat horizon.

The streets were strung in new prospect to Vesalius. He seemed to be walking above a flat dimension with the sun's globe impaled above a single-layered surface. He was an observer, an air balloonist, floating along a checkered, angled matrix. He could see shadings, nuances, details in new contrast. He could see more, much more of everything, more, even, than he wanted to see.

Vesalius crossed several streets. Even though his head swam, he'd decided to walk home. Offices had not let out yet and the people who were about must have been on some particular errand. Besides, traffic was light, the grinding gears and squawking horns would come later. None of it bothered him now; in fact, the whispering tires added to his detachment. To Vesalius, the street, its occupants, its machinery fused into a syrupy flow where the components stayed motionless in regard to each other.

He passed through a green-planted square, moving onto the tailored lawn in relief from the pavement. The grass was matted and very thick in spots, excellent hiding for acorns dropped by the oaks that dominated the square.

Vesalius slowed his pace as he walked through the square. His giddiness left him, filtered out by the different air of the greenery. He could no longer hear his footsteps, but his sense of detachment, instead of increasing, was now strangely diminishing. Then it came to him. He'd ceased being an observer in the grim events of the past days and was becoming part of them. Shadings, values and positions all had changed. He was in *process*.

Vesalius grew amused at the thought. Like so many men of refined passions, Henri Vesalius learned at an early age to hold people and circumstances at a distance. He could not endure animation in others, in himself even less. Of course emotions were painful; he shunned their possibility as much as he could. Like a miser, he trained himself to measure what little reserve he possessed against any anticipation of satisfaction. A love affair at twenty had left him desolate. The lady was too pure, too unassailable. His family sent him to Italy to clear his thoughts and breathe the Renaissance air. Venice stank, the rat-infested canals clogged with Swiss and German housewives. Turin was a vulgar industrial wasteland, uglier under the southern sun than its bleak Midlands counterparts. At Ravenna he visited Dante's grave—and fled. Rome, the Eternal City, was worst of all: by day its piazzas were staging grounds for hordes of religious petitioners, at night the panderers and their marks held sway. Most repugnant was the Sistine Chapel, its famed ceiling appearing to Vesalius like some clogged charnel house. He left Italy after only eighteen days of a proposed ten-month exposure to its "culture" and civilization, grabbing the first Mediterranean packet he could find out of Civitivecchia. He landed in Ajallid the next morning and, finding this inhospitable place to his liking, set out for the interior where he spent the balance of his trip earning the polished disinterest of the Corsicans.

Thus fortified by his prolonged exposure to indifference, Henri Vesalius returned to London, ostensibly a seasoned young man, newly ready for the rigors of his studies. He promptly met and seduced the young lady whose barrenness had caused his exile, only to equally rapidly discover that his earlier fervor was unwarranted. He left the seduction bed, if slightly dissatisfied, a confirmed ascetic.

But enthusiasm, or rather those circumstances that gave rise to it, on those rare occasions that it occurred in Henri Vesalius' life, came very slowly indeed. He walked through the square now and recognized the symptoms: the giddiness, the attenuated concern, the prolonged animosity, were all part of a train of events which he would shortly have to accommodate. His anticipation—for that was the central cause—came not so much from an eagerness to help snare the killer of his colleagues (he detested sentiment), but rather from his perception that a genuine emotion was at hand and, further, that he was about to permit himself to experience it. That emotion was fear!

By the time Henri Vesalius reached his apartments he was exhilarated. But rather than disturb Lem who was in the music room working on the new sonata, he decided to surprise the boy by whipping up an exotic supper. Father and son lived like bachelors and, the press of daily events being what it was, they dined out most evenings. But restaurant fare grew pallid after awhile, so periodically they treated themselves to a home-cooked dinner. Lem was more conservative, tending toward steaks and chops. His father had a penchant for bisques, pilaffs and omelettes. That night he would try his hand at sukiyaki, cooking it at the table in an iron skillet he had bought a week earlier especially for the occasion.

But first he would have to prepare the ingredients. He washed the rice and put it on the chromium-topped stove to steam. Then he washed the onions, beef, mushrooms and watercress, placing each separately on the wooden cutting block to dry. Then he unwrapped the beansprouts from the white paper the grocer had tied them in, washed them under the cold water and, liking their crispness, sampled a few. Still chewing the sprouts he chopped the other ingredients, transferring the piles to a breadboard with the edge of his butcher's knife. When he was done, he brought the board out to a low table in the dining room, where he'd stationed the iron skillet. Then he lit a thick candle underneath, poured in a bit of peanut oil and, selecting a pair of long wooden chopsticks, called his son.

The sonata swelled fluidly from the other room. "Lem, this won't wait. It's sukiyaki, come eat and finish that later!" Vesalius stirred the watercress into the hot oil. The green leaves sizzled and sent up a pungent steam that served to sharpen his hunger.

The boy came into the room. "Hello, Father, that looks good. I've heard about sukiyaki but never really tasted it before. Where do you find all these great dishes?" The boy poked a chopstick into the crisp vegetables in the skillet in which Vesalius was expertly stirring the slivers of beef.

"From secret sources which I'm honor-bound never to divulge. Now spoon out some rice for us while I finish here."

Lem measured two bowls full with a wooden spatula while his father continued stirring the sukiyaki which now, embellished of all its components, crackled fragrantly in the skillet. Vesalius added a final flourish by pouring a few drops of soy sauce from a crystal cruet onto the whole; then, inhaling the result for flavor, he began portioning the mixture into the rice bowls.

The result was absolutely delicious and they polished off the bowls without a sound. Lem was into his second helping when he was finally moved to comment: "It's great!"

"Glad you approve. We'll do this again, soon. But save room for dessert. I've bought some fresh pears."

"And a game of chess after that, Father? I want to give you a chance to get back."

"Let's play tomorrow night, Lem. I've got an appointment at eight with our new friend, Inspector Trout."

"Can I come with you, Father? I'd like to see the department at work."

"I'm afraid not tonight, Lem. We're going to meet at the Highgate Cemetery."

"What on earth for? I didn't think detectives went in for spooks and things of that sort."

"But they do like to check the facts. Say, excuse me for a moment, will you?" Vesalius cleared the utensils and returned from the kitchen carrying a bowlful of large comice pears, polished to a sparkling red and green. "I saw Mr. Darrow today."

Lem selected a pear and started to bite. "Oh, I'm glad you did that, Father. He is a bit old, and I don't think very many people come into his place. Interesting man, though, isn't he?"

"Yes, quite sharp indeed." Vesalius glanced at his watch. "It's seven-thirty. I'll have to hurry. Get back to the sonata now, Lem, it was coming along quite well."

He scrambled up from the floor, knees scissoring from the low position and strode with unaccustomed speed toward the front door. He grabbed his raincoat, which he'd left on the hall coatrack to dry and, calling over his shoulder that they'd try bouillabaisse next week, was out before the boy could say goodbye.

It'd been a long time since Lem had seen his father so

fired up. He hoped it would produce the desired results.

Trout was ready and waiting for him by the time Vesalius reached the vaulted entrance to Highgate Cemetery. The rain had stopped and the wind had torn enough holes in the clouds to let the thin moonlight through in intermittent bursts. Trout's black limo glistened fitfully as Vesalius climbed the low rise to the stone arches. He could see Trout's cigarette glowing out of the car's interior. It looked very businesslike.

"Is that you, Dr. Vesalius?" Trout emerged from the car alone.

"Yes, Inspector, the caretaker is expecting us. I see you've come alone this evening. Where is Sergeant Schenley?"

He joined Trout and the two entered the wrought-iron gate together.

"He's with his wife and family like any sensible man should be. Now what is it exactly this old man said?" The Inspector was brusque.

Vesalius could see that the detective did not like having his theories questioned. *Stuffy peacock*, he thought, looking slowly at the orderly rows of alabaster and granite obelisks, death angels, and plain slabs that spread in all directions from the gravel esplanade on which they were walking.

Their heels crunched the loose stones for several minutes. The wind had freshened and the sky was even clearer now. Of course the inspector was right. It was a far-fetched idea to come exploring acres of burial grounds after dark. They could just as well do it the next day. But there was something in the way old Darrow's voice had wavered that lent urgency to the project.

"Mr. Darrow may be old but he's not senile. He said the man buys music from him. It's worth a shot. If he's off-base, we'll find out soon enough."

"But the identification? Doesn't it seem a bit contrived to pull a name out of a hat? How can you be sure it's the same man?"

"Phibes is not a common name, Inspector. When I came across the name in one of my son's bibliographies, it was a simple matter to crosscheck it. The packet of old handbills proved the point: Anton Phibes did give an organ recital at Giffard's Theatre about fifteen years ago. Old Darrow knew him from the picture."

Trout listened to the surgeon in silence. They came to a stand of cypresses and stopped. The gravel split into several smaller avenues beyond that point, each one leading off into more rows of Gothic memorials stretched taut in the moonlight. A late churchbell tolled in the far distance: nine slow bells.

They'd been walking for nearly an hour across that funereal landscape but it had seemed a much shorter journey, perhaps because of the permanence of the place. Now they'd have to wait for the groundkeeper to take them on the final leg of their search. The churchbell stopped and the silence resettled about them. Trout lit a cigarette and began pacing about. "Maybe he's asleep somewhere," he said impatiently.

"He said he'd meet us. These fellows are usually

punctual." Vesalius scanned the gravel aisles again. "Ah, that must be him now."

A lantern bobbled along the path farthest to the right. This was narrower than the others and heavily overgrown with low branches and shrubs. The tiny light moved in a leisurely, serpentine fashion rather than holding to a straight course. Clustered along the avenues' edges hidden behind the dense overgrowth were the tall granite monoliths and fluted stone crypts of an older period.

"Hello. You must be Dr. Vesalius. Come, I'll show you to where you going. Although it's a strange time to be visiting out here." The caretaker whistled at them, his voice high and nasal from too many years of working close to the damp ground. He'd been a tall man once but was now bent and gnarled from age. He held the lantern in front of him as they walked, the curvature of his body shielding the yellow candlelight. Shadows surged and swelled along the sides of the path, which was so heavily overgrown in spots it was dark as a cavern. Here and there massive rough-hewn boulders slanted up from out of the shrubbery, their iron nameplates worn and nearly obliterated from age. At longer intervals the shrubbery parted into sloping alleyways that led deeper into rotundas. These clearings contained eight or ten crypts huddled together under stands of birches or elms. They reminded Vesalius of the bleak dead houses that lined Pompeii's crowded streets.

"It was good of you to come out, Mr. — —" Harry Trout broke the silence.

"Cadogan. Michael Cadogan's the name, sir. 'Twas no

trouble at all. My little shack's out yonder. The city fathers put me in charge here over twenty years ago after old Jarvis died. They told me to take good care of it and I could stay as long as I like. Even give me a little pension, they do." The old man wheezed with a quiver of pride in his voice.

"But you must get some help here, Mr. Cadogan. This is a pretty big place." Trout had to hurry to keep pace with the old man.

"Two hundred fifty acres. The old cemetery was opened in 1839. It was small, a tenth the size of what it's grown to. We have a crew of gardeners that comes in during the day. They do all the pruning and cutting. Then, of course, there's the diggers. Keeps the place pretty busy, it does. I just show people around, help them find the spots they've selected from the map in the main office."

"Which part are we in now, Mr. Cadogan?" Vesalius ventured.

"The old part. This here's one of the last sections completed. Mostly families who subscribed to buy the original piece of ground. Many folks moved their kin from the churchyards closer in to town. Hasn't been anything opened up here in fifty years."

"But there's been burials since then?" Trout probed.

"Only if they was members of the family. Otherwise a person would have to use the new section."

The three men slipped into silence, their heels muffled now by pine needles that had layered over the gravel. The sheer detachment of the place began to tell on Vesalius and he felt as if he'd been walking the morose granite avenues for months, even years. Trout walked a pace or two ahead of the others; he was anxious to get on with the job. The old man merely plodded along, his frame curved around the lamp; their only means of navigation. Abruptly he stopped at a thick archway formed by ropes of ivy that hung between two heavy pines. He stood before the arch and swung his lantern high enough to illuminate the cluster of crypts sequestered within. "You'll find it in there. First one on your right."

He swung the lantern again, this time high enough for Trout to see the lettering carved above the archway. There, hammered in Gothic type face, blackened and corroded by salt air, was the name "Phibes."

The caretaker turned to leave, but Vesalius stopped him. "Thank you for your escort, Mr. Cadogan, but tell me, will you be back to show us out?"

"No, I've other rounds to make, you know."

"But how will we find our way out?"

"The same way you came in," the caretaker shot back over his shoulder, then vanished into the darkness.

Then they were alone standing at the entrance to the cluster of death apartments. They waited for a few moments getting used to the moonlight, then made their way toward the Phibes crypt which, a bit lower and more imposing than the rest and embellished by rough-hewn granite trim in contrast to the others' smooth-polished surfaces, acted as an anchor for the grouping.

The door was heavy iron lattice which opened on well-oiled hinges at Trout's touch. Once inside he groped along the stone coping to find some candles. "We'd be lost without this lot," he said with obvious relief as he lit two, handing one to Vesalius. The crypt flared up before them out of its accustomed darkness. Three of the room's four walls contained spaces for caskets; these were arranged in five rows of five caskets each. Almost all of the spaces were occupied as shown by the nameplates.

Trout scanned the somber assemblage, peering first at the left wall, then the center, and then, finding nothing, turned his attention to the right wall. Gradually a geneaology unfolded: Orion Phibes, December 12, 1792; Eleanor Phibes, March 5, 1817; Marius Phibes, January 8, 1886, Katherine Phibes, February 24, 1890. Finally his light located what they'd been looking for on the bottom row. The brass nameplate was unmistakable: Anton Phibes, April 21, 1921.

"Right next to his wife's," Vesalius said in a hushed tone. "Let's take a look."

Trout put the candles on the stone shelving overhead and both men bent to the task. Gradually they urged the brass casket out from its niche but only after both had shoved and strained to get it moving. At last it was out.

Trout pried the lid open and lifted it upward, until its interior velvet straps were bent tight. "It's empty," he sputtered.

"Save for this." Vesalius pointed to a small silver box which shown dully in the flickering light. He reached in to open it.

"Ashes," Trout muttered when Vesalius had got it open.

"They don't tell us a helluva lot!"

"Except that someone was cremated in that car crash. The Swiss authorities have acknowledged that much." Vesalius sensed the hesitation in Trout's voice. "And . . . ?"

Trout accepted the gambit. "It's possible that those ashes are someone else's. His chauffeur, another passenger, or perhaps the car's remains."

"And that Anton Phibes is back in London."

"Your Mr. Darrow said it this afternoon." Trout smiled at Vesalius, then looked down at the space next to Phibes'. "Here, his wife's casket's been tampered with!"

Vesalius' eyes shot down at the place where Victoria Phibes lay. The stone drawer extended a hair's breadth from the wall and the dust around its edges had been swept clean. They slid it all the way out, then lifted up the top of the stately oaken casket. The coffin was quite empty!

It was well past midnight when Henri Vesalius got back to his apartment. And it was only when he'd shut the door behind him that he realized how cold he'd been. He went into the pantry and put the kettle on for tea. Maybe that would bring some warmth to his sod-dampened bones. He prowled about the cupboards for the tea box and was amused at how reassuring the stacks of brightly covered canned goods looked.

He and Trout had spoken very little after they left the Phibes crypt. Vesalius was loathe to advance any conclusions on their discovery, preferring rather to let the crushing gravel underfoot carry the weight of their presence in that largest of London cemeteries. Besides, he was certain that Trout would shortly, if he hadn't already, come to the same assessment: an elaborate murder-vendetta was in process of being stage-managed by someone close to the Phibes family. This was confirmed by the empty casket of Victoria Phibes and was certainly not denied by the ashes in that of her husband. That the stage manager—killer was too prosaic a description, Vesalius had decided—was a man of culture was evidenced by the modes of death he'd so artfully contrived and visited upon the four hapless doctors. That he was a man of considerable technical ability was demonstrated in his evident display of talent in poor Longstreet's dispatch. And, if he could work with the precision of a surgeon, he was also capable of the grand design. Hargreaves' death, staged in full view of a sizeable fraction of London's prominent, was achieved with a grandeur appropriate to the surroundings.

The teakettle's whistle brought Vesalius out of his musings. It had been a very long evening and his skin, still chilled from the gloomy excursion across Highgate, remained unwarmed by the tea which now steeped in the scalding water. He cut a piece of lemon and dropped it into his cup, letting it bubble for a bit before sipping the brew. Then he drank the whole cup slowly and with great deliberation, waiting for some warmth to return. Finally he turned the kitchen light off and went up to bed, still cold.

While Vesalius tossed in fitful sleep, the house on Maldine Square jounced and jumbled with the ripping chords of Bach's great organ concerto. The music towered and soared, billowing volumes into every reach of the house, sending a shiver into the very windowpanes with audible tone. Stairs and floors vibrated and draperies fluttered with the pounding, the roof channeling the sounds down into the darkened house like some midnight cathedral. But where the great baroque composer defined the dimension of godliness in men, the organist's rendition of the master's music this night possessed a harshness far beyond the composer's intent.

The music stopped and the source of its perversion became immediately apparent with the emergence of the Master of the Letter "P" from one of the countless main floor chambers on his way to another door on the same level; a door to the room which housed all the mementoes, effects and clothing of the exquisite creature who seemed to have captured his fatal affection.

This night he wore no cloak but was dressed in a long elegant sleeping jacket of gray silk quilted against the cold. His thin hair was combed back from his forehead, giving his long head a streamlined aspect. His bearing and poise bore the stamp of nobility. His hands, now ungloved, were long and tapered and gave full advertisement to his musical accompaniment. But it was in his eyes that confirmation finally came. Hard, intense, steeled, they left little doubt that this monumentally somber man and Anton Phibes were, or could have been, one and the same man.

But this evening he was far from pensive. The music, despite the death edge his hands had placed upon it, eminently contained all of Bach's zest. It was with that same zest, rather than remorse, that he entered the Shrine Room.

Once inside he moved to a segment of wall on which were artfully displayed a series of photographs of Victoria and himself. Content now, he looked at them carefully. In one they toasted the American writer F. Scott Fitzgerald. A second pictured Victoria, dressed in a dazzling short white rhinestone dress, doing the Charleston on top of a table, while Phibes applauded on the sidelines. With him was the then current Prince of Wales. Another photograph showed the beautiful couple dancing a stately pavanne at a lavish costume ball. That Phibes was a man of art was demonstrated by his choice of costume; elegantly outfitted in Napoleon's battle dress, he literally towered over Victoria, herself gorgeous in an Empire gown. A fourth photo held his attention longer than the others. It was a single shot of Victoria, dressed in an emerald green bathing costume, which offset her long reddish-brown hair and milk-white skin. She was reclining before a pool against a backdrop of fern and, in the stilled forest sunlight, spelled the full measure of Phibes' devotion. She was an odalisque!

From these reminiscences he moved to the beautifully inlaid dais beneath the woman's portrait and, glancing again at Victoria's image as if to discover a new shading of expression, began to arrange a bouquet of cut spring flowers in a Wedgwood vase on the dais. When the flowers had been plucked and pushed into a floral spray of considerable art, he applied a match to two incense-filled urns, sending smoke spirals about the portrait. Then he unfurled a long phono-jack from a portable console next to the dais and, plugging it into his neck aperture, knelt before Victoria's portrait in reverie.

He held himself in absolute silence this way for several moments, his flickering eyes index to his great concentration. The plumes of incense and the whir and hum of the equipment seemed to highlight his devotion. Then he finished and, reaching absently for another switch on the console, raised his eyes in withered despair to the portrait. Presently his voice, intensely harsh but strangely cultured, filled the room. His words, coming now from some mechanical process rather than his featureless face, were doubly poignant: "A thing of beauty is a joy forever." He began to weep, "How do I love thee? Let me count the ways."

He wiped away another tear. "My love, sweet queen, noble wife, severed too quickly, too cruelly from this life. I remain and suffer to bring delivery of your pain. Of fires drawn and memories met, soon we shall hold our two precious hearts in single time . . ."

He could stand it no longer and, groping again for the switch, shut off his mournful paean. Then he put his head down on the dais and sobbed, his shoulders low under a great weight of grief.

Chapter 11

MARK Kitaj was one of the best vascular surgeons to have come along in the decade. His brash brilliance often scored astonishing results considered impossible by the medical savants of the time. Neither a theorist nor a tactician, he was that rare breed amongst physician-scientists: an intuitive pragmatist. In the surgical amphitheatre, he was direct and totally practical; he made things work.

But he was a hack. A product of Sheffield and Oxford, he'd interned at Guy's Hospital under, among others, Henri Vesalius. It was at Sheffield that he developed a healthy interest in the research aspects of surgery, an interest that stayed with him during and through his internship. Among other things Kitaj perfected a technique for intestinal resection which shaved the standard six-hour operating time in half. Working with white rats, he first demonstrated their physiological compatibility to humans in a brilliantly executed series of studies. After that, he was able to work out the hemostatic techniques in six months. It took him almost as long to persuade the surgical director at Guy's Hospital to permit a clinical trial. Finally, over a great deal of opposition, he was given a chance to prove himself. That one chance was all he needed. The patient, a retired railway brakeman, was considered a dangerous surgical risk; had not a bowel obstruction threatened his life, he would never have been brought into surgery.

Kitaj's operation was a faultless demonstration of his technique. It earned him a standing ovation from the several hundred spectators gathered in the amphitheatre to watch him—at the same time that it earned him the deep enmity of the old staff members who had opposed him. The operation saved the patient's life and won for Mark Kitaj a measure of fame denied to most men.

But if young Kitaj drove hard at work, he was an equally driving man at play. He owned a yellow Stutz Bearcat that gave him more speed than he needed. He enjoyed horse racing, pursuing the thoroughbreds at Aintree and Epsom. Kitaj was an excellent handicapper and there was talk that he averaged 5,000 pounds a year from his work with the racing form. On those weekends he spent in town, his elegant small apartment in Kensington was the scene of intimate parties to which were attracted some of the more dazzling beauties on the social scene. He wore these women like jewels, picking them up one at a time for a period that never exceeded ninety days.

His current protégé was Audrey Basehart, a raven-tressed beauty of nineteen whom he'd met at one of the champagne receptions at the Grand National three weeks earlier. Audrey was an accomplished horsewoman, tall and reserved in appearance—qualities which immediately attracted Kitaj. After a period of conflicting schedules she contrived to visit friends in London for an extended stay. Geography and passion did the rest and the young couple managed to see each other nearly every day of her stay. This particular Wednesday she was waiting for Kitaj in his office-study at the hospital while he finished his morning's cases.

She'd come early so they could have a leisurely lunch. Then Mark was going out to Northolt Aerodrome for his first solo flight and she, squeamish about this new hobby, would visit the Tate Gallery during the afternoon. They planned to meet later that evening and go to the theatre.

Audrey's ruddy cheeks were in full bloom and her skin glowed from the excitement she'd known since meeting Mark Kitaj. Although she'd been formally introduced to the social whirl at her coming-out party and had been pursued by scores of apple-cheeked young swains, she'd known little of sensual pleasures. That wasn't for lack of trying by the young men in her life, or by young men who wanted to be in her life; for Audrey Basehart had all the attributes, and more, of those things considered necessary to feminine beauty.

At 5'7" she was taller than most other young women, in her sphere. Her black shoulder-length hair, which she wore loose or bound with a single gold rope, set her apart somewhat, but it was her carriage that gave her a distinction above others. She walked with long strides, literally throwing her legs forward in an evenness of gait that announced great determination. She looked neither right nor left when she walked but kept her eyes straight ahead.

Audrey was also purposeful, having mastered Russian while still in public school—and mastered it sufficiently to be able to correspond with a pen pal in Kiev. This young man expressed little personal ardor for her and filled his letters instead with his abiding devotion to chess and the poetry of Pushkin. Nevertheless, the letters caused concern, a concern which built into a full-blown rumor that "the Basehart girl" was being corrupted by a Bolshevik radical. Audrey enjoyed her notoriety immensely, refusing even to show the letters to her father when he demanded that she either clear up the rumor or break off the correspondence. She remained steadfast against all family entreaties and kept the growing stack of pale blue envelopes on her desk, protected by a red ribbon, to emphasize her decision.

Audrey's triumph came at her graduation when she delivered a paper entitled "An Enquiry into the Causes of the Great War" in which she excoriated the Hapsburgs, the Romanovs and the Windsors with equal spleen and precision. To no one's surprise but her family and friends, the paper was published in *The Observer*! Shortly after that, the young scholar, who was then hardly eighteen, was accepted at the London School of Economics.

She immediately confounded everyone by announcing that she planned to take a year off from school so she could prepare herself for the rigors of study by writing and research. She had just completed a draft on "The Economic Impact of the U-Boat Campaign on the British Economy in

1917" when she met Mark Kitaj.

The young surgeon's energy simply overwhelmed her. Like the scores of faceless young men who appeared at her home bearing candies and flowers with monotonous regularity, Mark Kitaj possessed all the necessary credentials to a successful career in the uppermost echelons of his profession. He was a bit older, it was true, but he was also different, markedly different. For while success was measured by where a man had been or could go, and by the collection of comforts he'd managed to acquire, Kitaj seemed far more interested in pursuing an idealistic stance. And in a profession that was, by nature, a group effort, he took great pride in his own work. It was this individualism, this precise attention to detail that fascinated, attracted, and quickly overwhelmed Audrey Basehart.

During the course of their short courtship, she'd felt her own reserve slip away and was amused to discover that its loss almost didn't matter. His initial letters to her were correct, models of decorum; they quickened her pulse not so much from what he said but by the fact that he'd chosen to write at all. He didn't *ask* her to join him in London. Rather, it seemed the right thing to do. Her parents, of course, questioned the propriety of the move but she countered their objections with assurances that she would spend most of her time completing arrangements for school.

Kitaj had sense enough not to pursue Audrey overtly. Their first meetings were subdued, amounting to little more than dinner at some of the better restaurants in the West End. On Wednesday mornings he served at the clinics, after which he was free the rest of the day. They used these afternoons to explore the great city, meeting at Westminster Abbey, at St. Martins-in-the-Field, at Cheyne Walk. Saturdays they enjoyed the programs at the Old Vic, and Saturday nights Mark showed Audrey off at a carefully selected round of parties.

They spent Sundays apart, she refusing to accompany Mark to the aerodrome to watch him practice his new hobby. Flying, which had been transformed from an art to a science by the War, had become fashionable, even popular in the post-war years.

Mark Kitaj had been flying for eight months, having learned on a Spad Trainer. After mastering the rudiments, he graduated to a de Haviland DH4. Because of the confinement and controlled tensions of the operating room, his air trips were like electric discharges. Sundays he went to Northolt regularly, almost religiously.

He'd been going only a few months when his instructor, a veteran named Cunningham, told him he would be able to get his solo in less than a year's time if he could spend a few more hours each week in the air. Kitaj accepted the challenge with his usual thoroughness. Wednesdays found him in the noontime traffic after spending six hours in the surgical clinics or ampitheatre. He was usually revved up by 1:30 and, with even the smallest assist from the weather, could log three or four hours during the afternoon. In seven months he was flying with a verve and assurance that few wartime pilots achieved, and Cunningham pronounced him ready for his solo with blessings.

Audrey, sportswoman that she was, would have no part of the young surgeon's enthusiasm for flying. In conversation, she maintained that she was too involved with equestrian etiquette to develop any appreciation for aerodynamics; but secretly she knew that she'd be too frightened ever to accompany Mark to the aerodrome—a fact she'd never admit to him.

The dashing surgeon brought the first intimations of love into Audrey's young life. She knew this and wisely let the process take its course.

For his part, Mark Kitaj was above such inducements. He was comfortable, awfully comfortable with Audrey Basehart, but just that—and nothing more. The fact that he was a gentleman would vouchsafe his treating her well. He would leave her with more than he found her.

One particular Wednesday morning he cleaned up quickly after a routine three hours in the surgical pavillion. He'd worked with Bernie Schwarz, a muscular Dubliner who had almost as much speed as Kitaj did. He and Schwarz had roomed together for a year at Sheffield but had lost touch when Schwarz went back to his native Ireland to complete his medical studies. They'd met by chance a year earlier and were now renewing their acquaintance.

"Why don't you and Audrey join Lisa and me for lunch?" Schwarz shot at Kitaj over the large steel washbasin.

"Not today, Bernie, me bucko. Today's my solo." Mark gave a final flourish with the green soap, spraying the air with flecks of suds.

"You're kidding! You just started a few months ago. Now I know what you've been doing all these weekends. And here I'd thought you'd gotten serious on us."

"I am serious. It's the ladies who aren't. They want a rose-covered cottage and baby and three months on the continent within a year. And where's there room for thee and me?"

"We're the breadwinners, Mark, or don't you read those ladies' magazines? You know a contented man should be sent off to work with a balanced breakfast and greeted with kisses at the door."

"I'll take what comes after. And leave the rest up to the chaps who write that drivel."

"The whole lot of it is done by maiden aunts. At least that's what my friends in publishing circles tell me." Schwarz winked and threw his towel into a hamper.

"Who wouldn't know what to do with a man if they got one in the parish rummage sale." Kitaj discarded his long green surgeon's smock and, rummaging about inside his locker, put on his shirt and began to knot his tie. "Tell you what, let's meet for drinks tonight. Audrey and I planned on the theatre. We can celebrate and make a foursome out of it."

Schwarz grinned. "Audrey again. For an independent man of leisure, there's one young lady who knows where you spend your time. She must be doing something right."

"She hasn't done anything wrong. Besides, she has a purpose in life. Other than the obvious one."

"And she's brilliant and beautiful to boot. You're beginning to sound like the rest of us. When're you going to pop the question?"

"When she corners me with her father's bank statements." Kitaj snorted. "Seriously though, we're really quite unserious. The young lady has her studies. And I have my work."

"Aha! That's just it. You have your work but it doesn't have you."

Kitaj was annoyed. "What're you getting at Bernie?"

"Not all that much and don't look so alarmed, Mark. But your eyes do have that distant stare. . . ."

"Oh, come off it!"

"And your hands move a bit faster. And your pulse speeds up. And when the end of the day comes: zowie!"

"Stop before I run you out of here." Kitaj threw his towel at Schwarz then started to chase him. Schwarz dodged behind the sink, laughing.

"See, I told you she'd gotten under your skin. But relax and let it happen. It's not such a bad feeling, after all; and you couldn't have found a better girl."

Kitaj returned to his locker and began putting on his coat. "You're reading too many of those magazines yourself, Bernie. Real life isn't just letting things happen. It's push and shove, a bloody snakepit, a jungle. If a man doesn't make things happen, he's not a man."

Kitaj grew pensive. "A man doesn't have all that much time and certainly damned little to waste on 'feelings' or 'thoughts' or 'intuitions.' Nobody ever asked William Harvey what his 'intentions' were in studying veins and arteries. Why? Because nobody was around who could ask the question. But Harvey went right at it, got precious little acknowledgment for his work too, and when he was finished, he and subsequent generations knew quite a bit more about what keeps us going!"

"But Harvey was a genius, Mark."

"With one difference. William Harvey was a genius who had the push himself—and let's emphasize that 'himself.' How many brilliant bastards do you know who've been content to sit on their duffs reading manuals and practicing medicine by rote?"

"Now that you ask, too damn many."

"Precisely. Jerzy Kaminski, that Polish chap we knew at school, knew more about tropical medicine than the whole bloody department. Where d'you think he is now?"

Schwarz threw up his hands.

"He's a fat OB-Gyn man, languishing out in the West End in a three-room suite that's something out of *Vanity Fair*. His office looks more like a ladies' wig parlor than a physician's workroom. And those women! Snivelling society brats in their £100 creations, looking like a bunch of ripe rutabagas."

"Where'd you find poor Kaminski out?"

"He rang me up some months ago out of the blue. Invited me to an office reception. In a fit of sentiment I made the mistake of going. So help me, he was celebrating the installation of a new tilt-table. He even went far enough to demonstrate it—with his nurse!"

"Good Lord, I hope she was pretty!"

"She was old enough to be a retired nanny. And even

then the old girl clung to her modesty, insisted on wearing the examining smock throughout. He had her perched up there like a prize pickle."

Schwarz started to laugh. "Did the doctor demonstrate his technique?"

"Of course. Tapped her knee, moved the levers and she opened just as if she was ready to breach a set of twins."

Schwarz roared. "No, he didn't!"

"Yes, he did. Veins and all. It was a spectacle. Immediately after, he served punch and cookies."

"Well, at least he observed the social amenities."

"Which is probably a fitting epitaph for Dr. Kaminski— a man that should've been."

"But you just said he had his three-room suite in the West End."

"Plucking his manicured hands into those overripe plums when he should be in Kuala Lumpur doing something about cholera."

"I see! The altruist speaks. You want this poor fool, who probably didn't have much to begin with, to sell out the few comforts he's worked—and worked like hell, as a matter of fact—to earn. You want him to give up the shined shoes, that one new suit a year, the linen table with the pretty wife's indifferent cooking spread on it every night. You want him to give up the bright-eyed kids, even that West End suite, to go where? Kuala Lumpur! To rot in a thousand square miles of steaming jungle, that's where!"

"But you've missed the point."

"What point? He'll go and rot to make some notations

in flimsy notebooks that maybe, if we're lucky, somebody else will be able to decipher in a decade or two."

"Cholera kills one-hundred-thousand souls annually. Kaminski was doing original work. Chances are that he could have had the disease licked, and also . . ."

"Say, Doctor, we'll take on the universe next. I've got to get along to pick up a young lady for lunch. And you have plans too, I believe." Schwarz cut the conversation short and got ready to leave.

"Yes, I've got plans. Today's the solo, you know. As soon as I get it, I'm going to convert you to a believer."

"Not on your life. I'll go as fast as I want right here on the ground. At least in an automobile I know where I'm heading."

"And you have only half the fun of getting there. Just one flight into and through those clouds would convince you, Bernie."

"No, thanks." Bernie shook his head emphatically. "Say, Mark!"

Kitaj looked up from his briefcase into which he was stuffing books.

"Good luck!"

Kitaj nodded. "Thanks, Bernie. See you later for drinks."

The door closed and Kitaj finished arranging his books in the old leather case. Then he tied the straps and was amused to see that his hands were shaking.

Chapter 12

AUDREY was alone when Kitaj got back to his office. She was sitting on a tall stool, half-turned so she could look out the window. Her cheeks were flushed from the sunlight and her brown hair shone softly. She seemed deep in thought, her high collar, piled white and lacy about her throat, giving her a slightly scholarly look. She wore a rose-colored cameo on a black ribbon, which showed just above the lace. Her hands were folded quietly in the gatherings of her long, black woolen skirt. Her plain clothes only accentuated the vivid colors of the girl herself. In that warm midday light, she was like a Renoir painting, a very beautiful one indeed.

"Have you been waiting long?" Mark was attentive.

"Not too. Sally and I had a late breakfast. She likes to stay in bed after Charles leaves and I caught up on my reading."

Kitaj smiled at her. "That's a fine pin. Is it very old?"

Audrey looked down at the brooch at her throat. As she shifted her gaze away from the window, her eyes seemed to film over. They looked dreamy and soft under her long slanted lashes. "My grandmother gave it to me. It's a likeness of her mother."

"So we have her to thank. What was her name?"

"Eustachia. Eustachia Vincent. Lionel, her husband, went to America right after my grandmother was born. He was a clerk in a dry goods store but the sea had gotten to him."

"He sounds like a romantic."

"Not entirely. There'd been a business setback here and he wanted to repair the family fortunes. He managed to scrape enough money together for passage. A few months later he wrote that he found work as a Boston whaler and that he'd booked on a vessel headed for the waters off Peru. That was the last my great-grandmother heard from him."

"How sad. Did she remarry?"

"No. Eustachia raised the little girl single-handedly. The shipping company awarded her an annuity so they were comfortable enough. My grandmother always said that the experience built up her mother's character; Eustachia was just nineteen at the time, her husband had been but 30." Audrey lifted her chin as she spoke.

Mark was impressed by her forthright manner. She was even now showing the magnificent womanliness that seemed inbred into her family. He could, had he been so disposed, easily find reasons for extending their acquaintance beyond the prescribed boundaries.

"How was your morning?" Audrey shifted to face him more fully.

"Routine. A stockbroker; the poor devil apparently has a wife he doesn't need. We patched up his stomach but he'll have to leave either the cocktails or her alone."

"Was her cooking that bad?" She pursed her lips.

"Oh, no. Not that at all. His ulcers are caused by worry which comes from many sources, including the usual haggle on the job and aggravation at home. For people on the way up, such as this stockbroker, ulcers are an occupational hazard."

"Is that the price of brilliance, Dr. Kitaj?"

"Only for those with faint heart and shallow competence. The really great seem to be able to take it all in stride. They live with disdain and die with energy. King Harold was struck down by an arrow, Shelley drowned, Caesar was knifed by his colleagues, Napoleon was consumed by cancer."

"You speak as if it's nobler to die in a violent fashion."

He thought for a moment then began to pace about. "I suppose you could say that, although perhaps I'm not really in a position to speak objectively about the ways of death. A physician is, after all, a biological craftsman. He assists life, or at least he's supposed to."

"At a pretty handsome fee."

"Yes, but when you figure the years a young man must invest in the profession, his compensation is in line with the rest of the economy."

Audrey grimaced. "Oh, Mark, I don't want to talk about those esoteric things. It's you I'm worried about"

"How's that?"

"Well, it's the airplane." She dropped her eyes. He could see that she was quite agitated. "It's your first time alone."

He stopped pacing, touched by her concern. "So that's what you wanted to talk about! You're worried about my solo flight."

"No, it's not that at all." She was murmuring now.

"Yes, it must be. You're blushing. Has it really upset you?" He put his hand on her shoulder.

"Oh, Mark." She looked up but once. He bent his head and brushed her hair with his chin. Then he kissed her forehead, her eyelashes, her nose, and her cheeks. He lifted her long hair in his hands, drawing her face closer with great gentleness and kissed her once, twice, again and again, softly brushing her hair, cheeks, eyes, with his lips. He could see the part in her hair and smell her perfume. Her lips were wet now, moist from his.

She murmured and he caught his name between sighs. She whispered, but he didn't want to hear. Her head turned from side to side, her eyes closed and her long lashes almost touched her cheeks.

He kissed her eyes again, brushing one then the other, then again and twice more. Her breath came in small gasps. His hand moved in the air, searching for something. He was standing very close to her now. His hand found her waist, then both hands circled her body and he bent down towards her mouth, found it waiting, turned up in the air, turned up to him. He pressed down, kissing her lips, her throat, kissing the white horizon now aglow. His hands remained around her waist. She sighed, breathed deeply; his hands held.

She moved, covering his face with her perfumed hair. Now she was pressed tightly against him, her hair covering him, her mouth at his, purposeful, pressing, moving, pressing deeply. She kissed him, kissed him, again and again. She was surrounding him, overwhelming him, her mouth against his.

He groped in the air; he edged back, bending further backward. He almost slipped. She was still kissing him, swarming over him. She'd opened her blouse and was moving his hand inside the white silk, open now beneath the rose brooch and the black ribbon. She was soft, so soft, except for the firm pink nipples standing erect.

He was breathing hard, feeling her body drive into his. She kissed him again. He could see her nude breasts, full and pink. He was bent backwards, with her above and over him. He was pressed back down, surrounded by the incense of her hair. He was against the ledge, losing hold, her breasts, freed from the white blouse, thrust into his chest. She moved against him, swaying in a steady rhythm.

"Time to leave." Somehow he had broken away and collected himself.

"Now?" She kissed him again.

"I must go," he said.

"Where?" She was still close to him.

He turned his head. "I won't be long."

She kissed him, more lightly now. "Please stay."

"We'll have this evening." He was moving from her. He kissed her forehead and kept moving away. She held him, but quietly. They stayed together again, waited some long moments, then he got up.

"Mark!"

He was putting on his coat. She gathered herself.

"A Dr. Vesalius called. He called a few times this morning while you were in surgery. I promised faithfully I'd get you to call back."

She was all right now. After all, they'd be together in the evening. He brushed her forehead. "Never promise anything faithfully." He thought awhile. "Vesalius? Vesalius? Good God . . . haven't seen him in years. I interned under him."

"I think you should call him. He seemed terribly anxious."

Kitaj laughed and moved to the door. "Probably remembered something he forgot to teach me. It'll have to keep. I'm late already."

He returned and kissed her lightly. "I'll call him this evening. Right now I've got my first solo coming up. Think of it!"

She gave his hand a final squeeze. "Good luck, Mark."

"Later, darling." He was out the door before she could say goodbye.

While Mark Kitaj raced out to Northolt Aerodrome, a less-than-cordial interview was taking place in the sedately furnished offices of Sir John David Crow. Like most top administrators with the Police Department, Sir John shunned publicity. He kept his public appearances to a minimum, preferring to attend to the department from his green-wallpapered suite of offices. The offices were located at the end of a seldom-used corridor on the seventh floor of the rambling Metropolitan Police Headquarters—a perfect hiding place. To Sir John, the cardinal principle of detection was invisibility; and it had paid off with a better-than average record of success during the years of his tenure.

In practice, Crow was not so much the master sleuth as he was the organizer. He marshalled his forces, shifting assignments to meet the changing texture of each case. He loathed grandstand tactics and used his men parsimoniously. As a consequence, he placed a great deal of responsibility on his subordinates and came down hard on them if their performances didn't meet with his expectations.

Now he pored over the blue-bound memorandum on his desk while Harry Trout waited beyond its clean-swept expanse. Sir John scowled then started to intone:

"Thornton . . . Dunwoody . . . Hargreaves . . . Longstreet . . . Hedgepeth." He pushed the report back onto the blotter then glowered at Trout. "I should have been apprised earlier."

"I did notify you, sir, in my report of May 10."

"In which you presented me with a gaggle of gibberish about dripping vampires and a murderous bee swarm. Do you realize what you've got here, Trout?"

"Sir!"

"Five of this city's leading physicians have died under questionable circumstances within a fortnight. The medical societies can't help but take notice; that is, if they haven't already. And you know what comes after that, don't you?"

"I've kept the press from getting involved."

"But for how long, Mr. Trout?" Crow thundered. "Doctors are more clannish than gypsies. An attack on one is viewed like an assault on motherhood. I don't propose to belabor the seriousness of the situation, but if and when the press does get hold of it. . . ."

"We'll have a disaster on our hands."

"Where the hell do you think we are at this moment?" Sir John picked up the report once more and threw it across at Trout. "A menagerie for a murder weapon and a motive right out of the de Medicis. If we don't handle this with kid gloves, the inquiry will go right onto the House floor. The whole thing is a political time bomb, d'you know that? And the last thing this department needs, Mr. Trout, is politics!"

"I understand, sir."

"You understand! Well, what the hell are you doing about it? If your theory's correct, you've got a bunch of built-in victims." Sir John fumbled through the report again, stopping at a page. "Whitcomb . . . that nurse, Allan . . . and a Doctor Kitaj." He slurred the name, pronouncing it phonetically. "Are you on these people?"

"We're making contact, sir. Schenley's working up the details in my office."

"And what're you doing in here? There's a madman out there and I want him brought in NOW!"

"Yes, sir." Trout saluted, exhibiting an unaccustomed display of obedience. He was painfully aware of his still precarious position with his chief. He removed the offending memorandum from Sir John's view and without pausing for further instructions, backed away from the green expanse. He made good his exit while Crow still glowered beyond the hurricane lamp at the far end of the room.

Tom Schenley was busy at the blackboard when Trout got back to his office. He'd blocked the board with a matrix and was plotting the addresses and work habits of the remaining probable victims.

"We'll have to lay it on them now, Tom," Trout said as he came in. "The old man is a bit upset. Sounded as if we'll pull the shades of hell down about the department if we don't get this thing solved in time."

Schenley kept writing his figures. "I thought he wasn't interested in this case, sir."

"I think he's afraid. He's worried the doctors will get on his back and we'll have the politicos nosing about. Definitely doesn't want the press into it."

"You can hardly blame him for that. But he can't say he wasn't presented with the facts . . ."

"No. But if he read half the material that crossed his desk, he'd never do anything else. What've you got here?"

Schenley turned back to the board and pointed at the columns of names and figures as he talked. "Five of the nine members of the surgical team that worked on the wife of Anton Phibes are dead. They've succumbed at the rate of one every other day for the past ten days, starting with Dr. Thornton's death on the sixth of May. Of the four remaining persons—and we'll start with the lady—the nurse Merill

Allan is at Middlesex Hospital where she also resides; Henri Vesalius is at the Burgoyne Model Works in East Ham where he purchases supplies for his collection on the third Thursday of each month."

"A punctilious man, that." Trout nodded. "Please go on, Tom, don't let me disturb you."

"Thank you, sir. Dana Whitcomb is another matter. He, perhaps the least' dedicated' of the lot, has a lot of free time on his hands. In a bit of cursory checking, we've found him to possess entree to at least half a dozen young ladies' apartments. And, if I may paraphrase the medieval wit, he seems not to go there for medical consultation."

"But where is he now, Tom? Six-to-one is not the most favorable of odds."

"Your question is quite appropriate. With our stringent manpower allotment, we've had to rely on irregular sources for much of this information. And we will continue to do unless the illustrious Sir John grants some new favors." He paused, then continued. "Dr. Whitcomb is currently localized at 186 Uxbridge Road, where he is probably cavorting with that apartment's occupant, a lissome maid from Denmark who had visited our Lothario not two weeks ago seeking employment."

"He moves fast."

"You would too if you could see the young lady. She is a dish!"

"Decorum, Tom, decorum. A detective never intrudes. Now what about our fourth candidate?"

"Mark Kitaj is a tremendously capable young surgeon

who works more than one might expect; he regularly puts in a half-day on Wednesday either in the clinics or in surgery."

"Sounds dedicated."

"'Aggressive' is the better word for it."

"I presume he works the other days of the week too."

"Diligently. He's built a paying practice and conducted several outstanding surgical demonstrations during the five years he's been out of medical school. He's a bachelor, young, good-looking, with a reputation as yet unsullied by personal enmities."

"And where is he on Wednesday afternoons?"

"We don't quite know yet. He leaves the hospital regularly about the noon mark but the car he drives is a bit too fast: he's simply lost us these past two Wednesdays."

Trout was disturbed. "Well, I suggest we find out." He reached for the telephone. "Where does he work?"

"Guy's Hospital."

Trout called the switchboard. "Susan, be a dear and get me Guy's Hospital. . . . Hello. My name's Trout. Detective Inspector Trout of the London Municipal Police Force. We're trying to locate Dr. Mark Kitaj of your staff . . . Yes, I understand he's gone for the day." He grimaced at Schenley . . . "but can you tell me his whereabouts . . . No, there's no problem, but the man may be in some danger . . . A private office . . . Thank you, I'll call that directly."

Trout hung up and immediately dialed again. "Yes, Susan, it's me. Get me ECkley 415 . . . Hello, is this Dr. Kitaj's office? This is Inspector Trout, London Police . . . No, nothing's wrong but we'd appreciate it if you could tell us where we could reach Dr. Kitaj . . . I see . . . yes . . . he's at Northolt Aerodrome . . . Thank you, miss."

Schenley was a bit surprised. "Northolt; now what would he be doing out at the aerodrome?"

"That's what I want you to find out, Tom. The girl in his office seemed alarmed. Get out there as fast as you can. And I'm going to see Vesalius."

Chapter 13

TOM Schenley negotiated the fifteen kilometers out Western Avenue to Northolt Aerodrome in just under fifteen minutes at full siren. Even then he was late. A small one-engine trainer was easing on to the strip on the far side of the field. Schenley could tell by the plane's stiff movements that the pilot was new. Two biplanes were ahead of him, revving up to take off. Schenley turned the siren full up and jammed his foot to the floor; the police limo jolted into full throttle on the bumpy approach road.

Northolt had been a training field during the war and still had a drab, efficient look. A cluster of low utility buildings huddled around four hangers which, in their camouflage stripes, rose like displaced hills out of the straw fields. A thin concrete "X" marked the utility of the place, the gray concrete streaked with rubber and oil from years of heavy use. The first biplane completed its approach and started to lumber down one of the runways, its wheels bumping the ground until it finally pulled up its nose. The second made its turn on to the strip as Schenley turned the corner of the long barbed-wire fencing and entered the aerodrome.

He could see the trainer in better detail now. The pilot was racing the engine and testing the ailerons and rudder. Twin plumes of blue-black smoke trailed out of its exhaust and the 300 horsepower engine was putting up such a racket that Schenley knew the pilot, seated in his open cockpit and caught by the full backdraft of noise, couldn't possibly hear his siren. Very quickly he shot the limo off the approach road over the open field in an effort to cut the trainer off. The limo bounced and shuddered as Schenley pushed it across the rough stretch of mown straw and dirt clods, its doors and springs shaking with the strain. He was approaching one of the concrete strips head-on when he caught the image of the first biplane at the edge of his vision to the right. He swerved and just barely managed to loop under the plane's landing carriage as it groaned overhead. That maneuver cost him the race, for when he next caught sight of the trainer the attendant was pulling the chock blocks away from the wheels. At that point Schenley was a half mile away.

Kitaj was totally absorbed in his machine. He completed his control check, took the signal from the attendant and pulled back on the throttle. The motor felt good, awfully good, better, in fact, than when he had old Cunningham in the cockpit with him. The power was all his now and he intended to use it full measure. He scarcely noticed the small black limo as he pulled back on the stick and pointed into the midafternoon sun. He wondered why the fool had his siren on.

At a point three miles away from Northolt as the crow flies, a sleek saloon car glided softly along a curving back-road. Its heavy grace was incongruous against the green hillsides as it crept with the tense compression of a tiger along a roadbed meant for wagons and little else. Its hood, which gleamed in high polish under the sun, bore the distinctive letter "P" in gilt Germanic block print.

The car moved around an S-turn and nudged softly off the road, pulling to a stop without the sound of brakes or, for that matter, without any sound at all. A young woman clad in a gray chauffeur's uniform piped in black leather got out and walked smartly back to the leather-strapped trunk. She was the same beauty who'd graced the ballroom of the mansion on Maldine Square a few days earlier. She looked disquietingly natural in this setting as she busied herself with the trunk. A few quick turns and she had the top open, taking out first a tripod, then a long brass telescope. These she placed expertly at the edge of a small roadside apron which dropped sharply downward to the valley below. Then she fetched a white stool from the trunk and set it at the base of the telescope in studied ritual. Finishing with that she returned to the car and tapped on the curtained rear compartment.

The valley that stretched out behind her was several miles wide. Alternate squares of green and gold noted the farms which led up to the low hills on either side. The only odd structure in the entire valley, other than a few hamlets, was the distinctive "X" of Northolt Aerodrome. This glistened like alien steel bands in the middle distance. Above, providing the only sound of the hour, were a few planes flying at the 10,000 foot level.

The saloon car's rear door opened against this distant buzz. Dr. Phibes, resplendent in a pure white hooded robe of pontifical length emerged with a flourish and strolled grandly to the telescope. A brass amulet dangled at his waist and his eyes were shielded by a pair of black smoked sunglasses. He took up his position at the tripod, a master of the situation.

Mark Kitaj made a few passes over the aerodrome and then set out on his flight plan. The schedule called for him to fly northwest over the Chiltern Hills to Oxford, thence south to Southampton on the coast and from there to return diagonally to Northolt, a distance of about 250 kilometers. Immediately as he reached cruising altitude the constraint of his nine months' preparation left him. It seemed as if the plane knew precisely what to do, that he belonged in the cockpit and that he could go anywhere and do anything he wanted to do. It was a novel, completely unexpected freedom that consumed him instantly. He thought nothing of his career, less of the social treadmill that had begun to impose itself on him. Audrey, gorgeous Audrey whose milky softness less than an hour ago had surrounded him, passed out of his thought like a day star. Only the sky was left, and the sun racing across the land.

He flipped out of his second pass and began the long straight run up the valley. As he pulled out of the bank, he felt a slight nip at his leg, followed right after by a sharper one. He looked down and saw a dull gray-brown shape dart into the floorboards below the instrument panel. A rat!

That was all he needed! Suppose the bugger bit into the control wiring or, worse still, got into the engine? Should he turn back? Mark hesitated for a bit then, thinking better of it, decided to stay on course up the valley. He leaned back as he pulled the plane up to cruising altitude.

At that moment he felt a sharp pain in his shoulder. He turned to find himself staring straight into the coal-red eyes of a fat, evil-looking wharf rat. The beast, absolutely fearless, was prepared to dig his teeth into Mark's shoulder a second time when Mark swatted him out of the cockpit to fall to a proper death nearly two miles below.

Kitaj was furious; he would have to speak to the Aerodrome master about the facilities. But at least the problem of his unwanted visitor was settled. He checked his instruments and was dismayed to find himself ten degrees off course. He put the trainer into a long left bank to correct the reading, gradually easing out of it as he got back on course. With that he noticed a spot of blood on his shoulder. The bugger had bitten clean through his leather flying jacket, and the cut would need attention when he got back. But he couldn't worry about it now, he still had some flying to do if he was to make Southampton by 4:30. And it was at least an hour for the final leg back to Northolt.

Suddenly he felt a grinding, scraping kind of noise beneath the flooring, the metal vibrating under his feet. He listened hard for a moment and, hearing no more, turned his attention again to the controls. With that the floorboards beneath his seat burst out, emitting a stream of oversize rats larger than the first. Grizzled and foul, they averaged two kilos if they weighed a gram. Even then they were lean, their ribs showing taut through splotchy fur. A heavy odor roiled up out of the floor with them, thick and fetid like a musky slaughterhouse. Then Kitaj saw the cause of the stench: flecks of fresh blood sprinkled their whiskers and mouths!

He counted six, eight, then a dozen of the beasts, and still the terrible grinding didn't stop. The floorboards wheezed with awful animation and the plane seemed to shake under its unaccustomed load. Kitaj spotted the reason for the disturbance: three of the beasts were jammed between his foot and the controls. In trying to kick them loose he'd been bumping the stick, causing the plane to move in a rocking motion. Very cool now, he recognized his danger; at the same time he grew furious at the senselessness of his predicament.

He had to do something, and do it quickly. He couldn't return to the aerodrome, and he couldn't continue the flight with a cockpit full of rats. He'd have to get rid of them by any means. He tore the straps open on the tool kit under the control panel, grabbed a long wrench and began battering the rats away from his legs. He couldn't hit them squarely for fear of damaging the controls, so he had to catch them with glancing blows. They squealed as metal thudded into flesh, then spun crazily with the blow's impact.

He managed to dispatch several in that way, sending the rest surging up under the controls. But as he bent to scoop up the last of his victims, it snapped out of its stupor long enough to bite him ferociously in the ball of his thumb. Kitaj moaned in pain, his glove filling with throbbing blood. Dizzy with agony he was quite unprepared for what happened next.

A thick blur shot across the floor and in a second a heavy shape, larger and more ghostlike than the others had attached itself to his wrist. He felt it gnawing, tearing at his leather glove, shredding it with teeth sharp enough to slit through metal. In the same blinding instant Kitaj felt the animal's teeth stab deep into his wrist, slicing through outer skin layers, through tendon and vein down to bone. His hand exploded in a violent quiver of pain, then went dull. The full dimension of this new crisis now came home to him: the rat had severed the ulnar nerve with the first bite. His hand was useless!

He looked down and could see the animal bite again and again at his hand which had dropped at a bad angle from his forearm. His glove was torn and here and there bits of bloodied flesh and bone protruded from the shredded leather. He tried to lift it away from the relentless teeth but the pain in the torn nerve ends of his wrist was excruciating. Just before he blacked out, he could see the animal still feeding on his dead hand.

He was awakened by a sharp stabbing sensation at his cheek. Without clearing his vision he swiped in the direction of the pain, focusing his eyes in time to see another rat go hurtling over the edge of the cockpit. Miraculously the small plane was still flying evenly, although it had entered a slight roll when he removed his good hand from the controls. There was no question now: he'd have to get back to Northolt. He jerked on the stick to right the plane before making his turn. He had to fight the controls to keep the plane from flipping over, all the while trying to pick up his dead arm to staunch the steady seep of blood into the dark pool on the floor. He was afraid of passing out again.

He'd just gotten the trainer's nose pointed away from the sun, and had spotted Northolt's hangers in the distance when he heard the scratching, this time sharper and more ominous than before, well up from the deep compartments. A cold surge of fear throttled him at these new grindings, and he had to force himself to concentrate on the controls. Other than his hand, which would need attention, he was in reasonably good shape except for a few scratches on his leg and face. He knew he could get the plane down safely; that left the question of reaching the aerodrome before he blacked out again.

The wind was now cold on his face and the motor was running smooth. For all the strains he'd put it through, the de Haviland was showing the kind of toughness that made it a popular plane for training. He set his controls again and opened the throttle full to take advantage of a tailwind. At that he hit a downdraft. The small craft dropped sharply and the plane was soon tangling to right itself. Kitaj strained with all the strength of his hand to steady the stick. With that, the scratching burst up again from the floorboards and another stream of gray shapes shot out from beneath the seat.

This time they overwhelmed him, climbing up the walls of the cockpit and biting his face and chest as well as his legs. He battered at them with his dead hand but only succeeded in knocking a few out of the cockpit. The others clung to his bloodied glove as he struck them, biting deep into the senseless flesh.

The animals were relentless, driven by the scent of his fresh wounds. They hopped and leaped at him at will. The plane was shuddering, and Kitaj knew he was rapidly losing control. Now he looked up to see the wings and struts crawling with the crazed animals. Just then he felt a horrendous tear in his thigh just below the groin.

My God, they've opened my leg, he thought in cold realization of his danger. He looked down to see the red spurts of arterial blood shoot out of the gaping wound. They'd severed his femoral artery!

Just before he passed out a second time he caught sight of the valley, tranquil far below in the afternoon sun.

Phibes watched the plane spin all the way down. It whirred like a compass needle without the true poles or a bird whose broken wings could no longer support it as it fought to find the air.

Vulnavia, his assistant, stood at the very edge of the promontory playing a white violin that was pressed clean and sterile under her jet hair. Had Phibes turned—of course, he didn't turn away from his observation—he would have seen her as he always enjoyed her: inchoate and pure of outline. She was a mannequin cut out against the long horizon.

But her presence and the music was enough for his purposes. She played a Glazunoff concerto, quite new. He'd taken a liking to the current music ever since he'd journeyed to Paris especially to hear a new piece by another Russian. "Le Sacre du Printemps" was not well received; the papers even said the audience was unruly, some used the word "riotous." But Phibes was ever to recall it as savage and exhilarating.

He bought whatever he could of Igor Stravinsky and of the Frenchman, Edgard Varèse. He wouldn't permit his orchestra to play the pieces and hardly attempted them himself. He preferred, rather, to have Vulnavia perform on the violin or piano. Initially his habit was to spend an hour or two a day in the music room where she would present a collection of pieces. Later on he enjoyed having her accompany him while he worked in his laboratory. He found the music appropriate. He permitted himself the thought that it enabled him to keep up with things "modern."

That day the Glazunoff violin concerto was eminently appropriate. It fed on the ripeness of the Russian soil and so blended well with the green-and-gold afternoon valley. It did not fit, however, with the spiraling aircraft now out of control. And Vulnavia stopped as soon as the orange-black plume announced the end of the deadfall.

Phibes turned from his telescope, his hands elevated in the triumph of some great field commander at the flush of victory. He hissed in his characteristic sardonic excess and his eyes darted and gleamed evil in the daylight. Vulnavia, always sensitive to his mood, stood at his side offering a champagne glass on a silver server. He lifted the crystal and, pouring the entire contents into the aperture in his neck with relish, bowed to the girl and repaired to the car.

The closed rear curtains of the saloon car signaled the end of its mission. It sped away from that place as silently as it had come.

The next morning Harry Trout's office was a maelstrom of activity. Sir John had been in first off to receive the report of Kitaj's death. Trout was surprised when Sir John didn't blow up. Rather, he admonished him that they would have to exert maximum security with the remaining members of the surgical team and told Trout to take whatever men he could find for the purpose. When he left, Trout confirmed a particularly resigned note in his chief's attitude, an observation which disturbed him greatly.

But he had little time to brood about it. Just after Sir John, Tom Schenley called to say he was bringing in a Miss Audrey Basehart. The young lady had called the dispatcher near midnight on the evening before to inquire about her fiancée's strange "accident." The call had been routed to Homicide where Schenley, who was just then completing his report, asked her to come in the next morning.

Trout was notably surprised by the girl's looks, but something in her reserve and the hollow patches about her eyes told him not to press the point. He kept the conversation polite and subdued to a fault, which fact drew a note of praise from Schenley who'd instantly observed upon introducing the two, that Miss Basehart and Mr. Trout would make a very fine couple indeed. Mercifully the interview was short, shorter even than Sir John's, and she left with a not objectionably lingering handshake and Trout's sincere condolences.

As soon as the door closed, Trout signaled Schenley to remain. "We're on the last lap, Tom. It's going to be all footslogging from here on in."

"You mean we're done playing catch up, sir?"

"Emphatically."

"I wish Sir John could have sounded a bit more affirmative."

"I thought it was a morale problem too and then thought better of it. What really happened is that he's giving us carte blanche."

"I'm afraid you read a bit too much latitude into the director's remarks, sir. What he did say was 'to take whatever men we could find,' if I may quote him, precisely. D'you know how that reads?"

Trout stared at him.

"Ten men from this division and thirty from the district stations, most of the lot on restricted leave."

"Forty men to provide security for three active professional people!" Trout was incredulous. "So that's what's behind that half-hearted pep talk. He's putting us in a box with the hope of crying poor mouth later. Does he think he can get away with that? The press will shoot it full of holes."

"He had no choice. There are at least two major cases on

the docket right now. And the disarmament sessions are taking all the reserves."

"But our people are going to need around-the-clock surveillance, stakeouts and personal guards as well as the tracking team. We can't produce them out of our hats. And surely by now it must be common knowledge that we're not dealing with an amateur!"

"What I saw at Northolt yesterday only confirmed the caliber of the man. Kitaj was dead *before* the plane crashed. The rats—and there must've been over a hundred parked in the fusellage, I don't know how the trainer got off the ground —had been starved for at least a week prior to their use, A dousing with fresh blood did the rest."

"But wharf rats aren't killers," Trout said.

"The blighters'll eat anything. It's the only way they can survive; and they've been known to attack infants in prams and winos that don't watch where they're sleeping."

"Well enough of that. You say Kitaj was dead before the plane crashed?"

"Quite! The rats disabled his right hand. Tore his wrist to shreds. He had all he could do to handle the plane. He'd only gotten about ten kilometers from the aerodrome when the first attack came. He knocked a few of the beasts off and then turned around for home. Cunningham, the instructor, says he could've made it: he was that good a student. But the rats went to him again. This time they got a deep artery too far up in his leg for him to put a tourniquet on even if he could have manipulated one. He lost consciousness just before he reached the aerodrome. They saw him crash."

"The filthy bastard!"

"The man's a demon. Probably feels he can't be stopped. But he's also a logical and quite conservative fellow. He hasn't veered from the timetable yet."

"That G'tach formula from Rabbi Ben Gabirol. Vesalius was puzzling on that one last night. The last curse— darkness —is a cropper." Trout pondered for a minute and then asked impishly: "D'you think our killer is going to pull off an eclipse?"

"I know he's pretty well set on pulling off these three remaining murders. You'd think he'd also be up on the odds he's going against. A professional would surely know that the more exposure he risks, the less his chances are of going undetected."

"Turn that around, Tom. They also get better for his getting caught, which is precisely what our Dr. Phibes wants."

Schenley started. "So you think the doctor put his ashes together?"

"We have almost no other choice. At least no other possible suspect who's currently viable unless some maiden aunt is stuck somewhere in the woodwork. But I'll have to go with the man who had a motive. And that man was the good doctor—which reminds me Tom, did you know he wasn't a medical doctor?"

"No!" Schenley's mouth gaped in surprise.

"He took his doctorate in physics at Cambridge, then went on to Vienna for further studies in music. His dissertation there consisted of a concise but detailed discussion of the impact of music and musicians on the feudal courts of medieval Europe."

"The man was a scholar, I'd say."

"And you'd be partly right," Trout agreed. "He also was a polished performer and was known on the concert circuit."

"With the Philharmonic?"

"That would be out of character. The doctor was a soloist. He played the organ."

"And the Foreign Service?"

"Phibes was already forty when he met Victoria who was seventeen years his junior. He loved her instantly and lavishly in a passion not uncommon to a man of his stature and position. However, he appeared to be sincere, and quite honorable in his intentions. So much so that he did not want to drive her away with the apparent aimlessness of his life."

"He was a profligate."

"Not really, but his family, Austrian originally, and well landed, placed no compunction on its scions about careers and the like. Other than his recitals and an occasional lecture to library groups, Phibes had done nothing in the way of work since leaving Vienna fifteen years earlier. His parents had both died since and, save for a few maiden aunts and an odd cousin or two on the continent, Phibes was quite free to drift. The only reason he remained

in London is that he'd grown accustomed to it during his schooling."

"A diffident bastard, I'd say," Schenley replied.

"But Victoria changed all that, Tom. Two weeks after he

met her he broke into foreign service, strictly on the force of his personality."

"Are you sure it wasn't a family connection, sir?"

The foreign secretary still remembers their first interview. He performed diligently, ably and absolutely brilliantly, showing a facility for 'handling difficult negotiations with dispatch,' or so was written in his evaluation. For her part, Victoria was the perfect match for this strange older man who seemed bent on courting her. He was quite handsome and, of course, quite well off. But the Devereaux family was wealthy in its own right; this plus Victoria's obvious qualities could have brought her any one of a dozen young eligibles who'd already paid her formal homage."

"She must've been a perverse girl. If she were my daughter I'd cane her for chasing the likes of Phibes."

"There's where you err, Tom, and not on the side of the angels. Victoria loved her doctor. She had the good sense not to let him know it too quickly. It was on her devotion that his career as well as their courtship thrived. Almost a year from the date they met, they were married at Canterbury by the Archbishop himself. The wedding was greeted with favorable, even glowing reactions in the press. And all doubts, even those of her family who'd resisted to the last, about the propriety of this union were dispelled."

"Sounds like a storybook finish. What went wrong?" Schenley asked.

"Nothing. If anything, Phibes' work improved. Reluctantly, he accepted assignments on the continent where his knowledge of history and economics could be put to good use in a research capacity. Phibes surprised everyone when he was principally responsible for the negotiation of a series of highly favorable trade agreements with the Russians and French."

"And their marriage?"

"It flourished, even swelled. Phibes' tastes brought him in constant touch with the literary and musical lights of the day. He especially seemed to gravitate to the American expatriate writers who were just then making a name. Dos Passos, the Steins, T. S. Eliot were all known to him as was Ernest Hemingway. The couple was, in turn, idolized, with Victoria's wit and perception making them favorites at the popular 'salons'."

"It's almost sad to hear it. A storybook courtship, a popular marriage, ending too abruptly."

"It sounds like the classical tragedy."

"And as such must have its final act of—if we can borrow the word again from the G'tach—retribution."

"Phibes couldn't accept that he'd lost it all. The best part of his life had been taken from him. He demanded payment."

"On a godly scale. And he's damn well going to pull it off. He's got enough bitterness to see him through worse than we've seen yet. Now where do we stand on our lineup?"

"Nurse Allan is most heavily covered because of the accessibility of the hospital. I've had staff in plainclothes both on the grounds and in the park across the street for the past two days, plus double guards on her floor of the Resident Quarters, as well as the floors immediately above and below."

"Good. I've been on Vesalius, although I must admit that the man is ornery enough to call himself 'resentful' of the imposition on his schedule. And Whitcomb?"

"We're taking him out of the country—that's if he'll come along."

"*If* he'll come along!"

"We've had trouble persuading him; claims his practice will suffer. Personally, I think it's that Danish girl. He's been spending his nights—and most of his days—over there."

Trout exploded: "Listen, Tom, you get him away from that little bitch if you have to threaten to deport her. He must think he's playing cops and robbers. Now you convince that fool of what he's into and tell him that I want him on the train tonight or I will personally see to it that he's placed in protective custody! Clear?"

"Clear as day. I'll get right on that now, sir."

Sergeant Schenley seemed particularly happy to accept that assignment.

Chapter 14

"ULLA!" Whitcomb called.

"Yes, Dana?"

"Don't call me that! I am your king. Say that. Or better still, 'My liege.'"

"But we aren't ready yet, Dana!"

"No matter. You must learn the value of the royal imperative. The king commands; his followers obey. If you are to be my queen, then you must always do as I say. You want to be a queen, don't you, Ulla?"

The girl hesitated, blushed and looked down at her long legs which were quite bare.

"Well, don't you?" he demanded.

Her plump hands twisted and knotted the lace handkerchief. She wore a gold filigree chemise and sat regally, if a bit forlornly, on a low white boudoir stool. Whitcomb was amused at the way she kept her eyes lowered. It was almost shy, adding to the poignance of the girl who'd positioned herself before the uncovered dressing table. *The little wench. Doesn't she realize the chemise scarcely covers the small of her back? She's trying to throw me off!*

Whitcomb thought, marveling still at the girl's voluminous posterior.

"Yes," she murmured.

"Yes what?"

"Yes, my liege."

"Again. Say it again so you'll have it perfect."

"My liege."

She was beginning to make a good pupil. "That's better, Ulla," he said.

"Sir!" she said, playing the game now.

"That's better, *my queen*! Of course the royal imperative must be served. Now tell me, who am I?"

"Edmund Ironsides."

"Perfect. And you are Ealdgyth. Ealdgyth, Queen of Mercia."

She lifted her eyes a bit.

"And of Anglia and Cambria as well," he added. "And if we can secure Gruffyd's fealty our suzerainty will extend into Northumbria."

"Oh, Edmund, I'm so excited. Think of it! Danelaw will become Mercian power!" She crossed her legs and Whitcomb could breathe the freshness of her thighs. The girl was better than the others, really "appreciating" her history. He would use her next week in the House of York ascension. And many times after that. But now they must perform the coronation, the final setting of his seduction.

"A strong and united England, ours to command. But there's still the question of Gruffyd. He came into East Anglia last winter and rumors have it that he's provisioned his army again against another season's activities."

She finished dressing and stood up, now clad in a short maroon bodice trimmed in lace and framed behind by an elegant red velvet train. Although she was but twenty, Ulla looked every bit a queen . . .

Whitcomb had met her at a gallery opening a few weeks earlier. He was impressed not only by her transparent spiritual beauty but by her appreciation for history as well. At the time he could not ascertain whether she was a schoolgirl who was caught up in the romance of history, or rather a discreet and highly sophisticated whore who, with a discerning eye, was able to sense the specific and rather elaborate predilections professionals tended to and was pursuing a career in their service.

During their acquaintance Whitcomb was never so gauche as to question the girl directly, much preferring to enjoy the stimulus of an extended doubt. He had little trouble in obtaining her key, considerably more in obtaining her favors. And when he did, his surmise of her virtue was instantly confirmed: she wept, pleaded, cringed and finally yielded to his sexual onslaught which Whitcomb, as he gloated afterward, did not have to feign for the first time in a decade.

Partly in pride, partly in self-remonstrance, he sent her a rose and brought her to dinner at Simpsons where Ulla's straw-gold hair and flushed skin dominated the large dining room for more than two hours. Also, to ease that part of his conscience which was still outraged, he refused to stay with her that evening. The next day a card in his postbox signaled her disdain and, incidentally, the end of his freedom.

Their second meeting was a reversal of the first. She produced a supper for two from out of a kitchen of the most modest appointments. Dinner was concluded with a dessert wine and good Brie cheese, after which they repaired to her canopied sleeping room without any urging on his part. Once there, he was subjected to such a silken assault that he found himself beating a tactical retreat on buckled knees at three o'clock in the morning.

Thenceforth Ulla, dear school maidenly Ulla, was someone quite different at each encounter. And these meetings, due to the fever in poor Whitcomb's blood, soon became daily affairs.

Poetess, priestess, muse, milkmaid, all these Ulla played with a drive and humor far beyond her years. She could be contrite, petulant, noble and scheming with equal fervor, exhibiting a range which spoke of an even larger repertory that would take months, even years to explore.

After one week, Whitcomb was testing the idea of marriage upon himself, this sentiment dissolving in his traditional cowardice after only a few hours of sweated contemplation. Relieved, he decided to offer her everything.

To his astonishment and in a gesture that immediately endeared the young girl to the aging playboy to an even greater degree, she declined to list all those things which would "make her happiest" according to his request. Instead, her RSVP suggested that they spend the very next day absorbing the stately architecture and historic impediment of Westminster Cathedral.

Whitcomb declined with regrets, suggesting that they postpone their outing until the weekend when he would be able to break away from the press of business. In fact, he'd scarcely worked a full day since they'd met. For that matter, his work habits were sufficiently sporadic and his practice had fallen to such a low estate that, had it not been for an annuity bequeathed to him by a long-since forgotten Aunt, Dana Whitcomb would be, if not penniless, forced to live on income.

Nevertheless, he lived high. And it was with characteristic aplomb that he sent a carriage to call for her promptly at 3 P.M. on Saturday, the time of their appointed meeting. She seemed properly impressed at his costume which, in keeping with the occasion, consisted of trousers cut from the tartan woolens of his clan above which he wore a sleek blazer bearing the flaming shield crest of the House of Whitcomb. Ulla wore white, and he would have immediately clasped his hands about her tiny waist had it not been for the purity of her composure. Instead, he kissed her politely on the forehead and then reclined into the soft cushions of the hansom, there to contemplate the ravages he would visit on the virginal girl after their ecclesiastic outing.

He entered the great and noble abbey bearing the splendid girl on his arm. He wanted to move to his right to review the stone markers of the great and near great that lay along the wall, but a steady and consistent pressure from Ulla's white-gloved fingers held him on a course down the great center aisle. For Dana Whitcomb that was to be a fatal mistake. For in their passage, the power long instilled into the stones by the steps of generations of British royalty now transferred into them. By the time they reached the vaulted altarwork at the cathedral's far end, Ulla's exclamation was almost an understatement.

"I feel so—so—queenly!" she breathed.

"You are, and shall be, my dear!" said Whitcomb, in calm command of his fervor which, even then, was threatening to bring sweat to his scrubbed palms. He hardly could have appreciated the dimensions of the promise the young Ulla found and permanently locked into his words. He decided they must have a coronation, complete with all the trimmings.

That very afternoon Ulla thought it necessary to make preparations for the forthcoming "occasion." The ensuing trip to Mayfair, in which the bemused Whitcomb steered her through a series of milliners each more elegant than the last, was concluded only after he discovered his checking account to be near the point of exhaustion.

Three successive days, with rounds of fabric selection, fittings and color coordination, accompanied by the interminable discussions with seamstresses or, worse, those purple young effetes whose presence was obligatory in certain salons, afforded Ulla with a collection of court gowns, capes, shoes and streetwear worthy of the Hapsburg.

The furnishings of Ulla's apartment came next, inaugurated by a purchase of a brocaded rug which, Ulla explained, was the only appropriate complement to the silken slippers which they would wear at home together. To match the rug, the rooms had to be repapered. At Ulla's urging, Whitcomb commissioned an embossed design that incorporated his family crest overprinted on a delicate scripting of their initials in gold. A commode, in the manner of Louis Quatorze, was bought with his last farthing. After that Whitcomb conducted his negotiations on credit. He loathed this action but was by that time so taken by the circumstances which forced him into it that he thought nothing of signing over documents granting a percentage of his income for the next five years to that last refuge of the profligate: a personal loan counsellor. With his bankroll newly, if shakily, bolstered, he was able to underwrite settees, chairs, odd tables and other companion furnishings to the commode. Ulla's apartment was beginning to take on the aspect, if not the expansiveness, of a baronial palace.

During this brief, but extraordinary spree, Whitcomb hardly had time to question his durability, so artfully did Ulla induce him into her service. And the one time that he gathered courage enough to ask her what she was about, her quick reply disarmed him totally: she wanted him to "instruct" her in the ways of the nobility.

From her remark flowed the final architecture of his innermost dream. Whitcomb, throughout his entire life, had considered himself as "to the manor born." And, although English schoolboys learned well the court life of their ancient rulers, the gloss and glory of these days never left his imagination. In his manner, dress and speech, he affected the ways of the court or at least what he fancied them to be. And in the tedium of his work, those minor victories when colleagues and clients inquired as to his lineage, were far more important to Dana Whitcomb than any praise for his medical craftsmanship.

Later, when his confirmed bachelorhood had transformed him into an amiable rogue and the need for increasingly elaborate settings to his seductions grew, he first fancied and then enacted the roles of judges, vicars, seneschals and dukes in a variety of boudoir settings. And the young ladies, each of them gorgeous and voluptuous in her own right, were variously bewildered, amused, even titillated by his prancings. But none save Ulla had ever exhibited the command, the daring, the sheer ability to counter his most cherished performance: queen to his king. And when he found her, he was prepared to give all.

They were ready now for the coronation, he in purple diadem, his graying locks polished and patted into place, and she in her elegant red train. They walked slowly to the Louis Quatorze commode in regal splendor. Ulla kneeled on a small white pillow and waited, her heavy lidded eyes closed in anticipation, her breasts heaving magnificently.

Whitcomb lifted a small black lacquered box. He had pawned certain pieces of his office equipment to purchase what was inside the box—a diamond-studded tiara. His hands shook slightly as he opened the box, hesitating at each small metal clasp. He lifted it out of its velvet container and placed it on Ulla's head.

They kissed in awesome hesitation, then murmured the venerated text of regal acceptance and responsibilities with salutary fervor.

His knee, through a dozen layers of garments, pressed close to hers. Their eyes locked in tearful emotion. He pulled her to him, and she yielded. In exultation, in joy, in relief, they leaped into the royal bed.

In the midst of their silken transport, a metallic "tinkle" announced callers at the door. They couldn't move—or rather could only move to one rhythm. The bell rang again. He shifted, his ankles protruding from the sheeting in exclamation. She pulled him to her. The canopy jostled. The outside door was pounded.

They moved forward, royally. He thought of Charlemagne, of Henry VIII, of Louis le Grande. She thought of him. They sighed. The canopy jostled. The front door shook.

"Sire . . ." Her eye opened underneath the coverlet, its violet pupil glowing like a night coal. "Someone is come." He muttered, his head was at Agincourt, his lady on Cleopatra's Barge. The knocking grew louder.

"Sire, someone is here and will not go away." She rolled her silk-clad bottoms and bit his ear.

"Call the guards," he mumbled, and caught the skin of her throat into his face to smother himself.

The knocking continued. The canopy shook, the battle raged.

"Sire, our castle is surrounded," she shrieked, even a little anxious.

"Then lift the drawbridge and sound the clarion. Who is it this time wench?"

"I am no wench, I am your queen."

Ulla attempted to rise, drawing the silk gown about her as she slid to the edge of the bed. Whitcomb spied her royal ruff in the process, and pulled her back.

"You are a queen, my queen!" He parted her gown and kissed her in the cleft of her chest, smothering himself in perfume. They slid back to the pillows again to begin the motion of the beast with two backs. The bell tinkled twice, thrice, the door pounded.

"Sire, the Normans have landed and march now on London. Duke William has come for his crown."

"Wot! He comes finally to defile the soil we've fought for so dearly. Assemble the thegns and housecarles. Call up the great Fryd. And ready my horse and train. We will march from Stamford and put sword to his folly."

Thus animated, a livid Dana Whitcomb clambered up out of the bedclothes where he'd just claimed one victory. Buckling a heavy chamois greatcoat over his naked flanks, he marched to Ulla's door. Undoubtedly, the bravery of King Harold was on his mind.

That the two men at the door were not in Norman mail gave Whitcomb pause. For their part, Tom Schenley and Corporal Peters were equally caught by the rotund figure of a man who now stood blinking out at them from the apartment's half light.

"Dr. Whitcomb?" Schenley inquired with forced gentleness.

The doctor seemed at first not to know his own name. Then the symmetrical cone of the corporal's helmet provided the needed tonic. Whitcomb patted his tousled locks, drew up in full measure of his long gown, and, rocking on the balls of his feet to gain height, addressed the callers. "Yes, I'm Whitcomb. But how do you know to look for me here?"

"We'd rather not go into that now, Doctor. May we come in?"

Schenley edged forward. Whitcomb shifted to block his entry.

"But I'm not prepared to receive visitors. Can it wait?"

"I'm afraid not, sir. Now, may we speak with you inside?" Schenley gestured to pass, then, almost as an afterthought, stopped and made the proper introduction.

"Pardon the oversight, Doctor. This is Corporal Peters, and I'm Sergeant Schenley, Metropolitan Police, Homicide Division."

Schenley could see that the doctor, like all law-abiding citizens, had set his mind racing as to the specific causes of their visit. But the urgency of their mission would permit only the barest of explanations. He addressed himself to this straightaway as they entered the lavish parlor.

"Dr. Whitcomb, several years ago, you were part of a surgical team that operated on a young and very lovely society woman. Within the last fortnight six of the nine members of that team have died, each one of a strange and, if I might editorialize, disturbingly violent cause. We have reason to believe that someone close to the woman, maybe her husband— although he is officially presumed dead—is directing this conspiracy. Or perhaps it is a diabolical if irrational prank. In any case we are under orders to provide maximum security for the three remaining members of the team until the killer—or killers—can be brought to justice."

Whitcomb had to steady himself, then sit down on the ochre-colored settee as the full force of Schenley's statements hit home. He also felt a tinge of relief that the visit was for that, and not some less savory purpose. He still secretly delighted at his recent exploits and fancied himself ever the Lothario: amoral, heartless and perhaps even disreputable. Just then Ulla announced her presence.

"Dana, who is it?" She emerged now from her bedroom enveloped in a long, white-lace wrapper that revealed to full advantage her purple stockings and a long expanse of golden skin unencumbered by any article of clothing whatever. "Oops," she tittered and dashed back into the darkness of the bedroom with a jounce of her flanks that left both of the policemen's mouths agape.

"Why, it's Ulla Siguroson," blurted Corporal Peters.

"D'you know her, Corporal?" Schenley eyed his partner.

"Not officially, sir. Just through another department. Frothingham over in—"

Schenley cut him short with a discreet cough. "You can tell me some other time. Let's help the doctor get ready. There's no time to waste."

Whitcomb had by now gathered whatever composure remained to him in his awkward circumstances and was able to express his first utterance of displeasure at Schenley's unannounced and, to him at any rate, unjustified visit. "Get ready! Surely, gentlemen, you can't be serious. I'm not prepared to go anywhere. I have my practice, my patients to think of." He gestured with an expansion far beyond the actualities of his business situation.

"Dr. Brockman has already consented to look after your patients for a few days. We will make other arrangements if more time is indicated."

"If more time is indicated! Where d'you think you're taking me? This is beginning to sound like an extended holiday."

"Not at all, Dr. Whitcomb. You're going to the country for a few days."

"To the country? Why on earth there? I don't know anyone in the country."

"But you must. Your friends the Woosters have invited you to their cottage in the Cotswolds."

"How kind. Of course, I haven't seen Enid and Gregory for eight months, but at least we can play cribbage." Whitcomb was getting frayed.

"Oh, they won't be there," Schenley said.

"Won't be there? Then why am I going to an empty house?"

"Security, sir. It's much easier to guard an isolated home in the country than to watch a heavily trafficked town apartment such as this."

Whitcomb balked. "I beg your pardon."

Schenley parried nicely: "Sorry, sir, I meant to say your own quarters as well as your office. Now, can we be going?"

Whitcomb grumbled all the way from Ulla's apartment

to his hotel in Marylebone. But he sulked merely to keep up appearances. His practice could hardly suffer by a few days' absence. It'd be a relief to be gone a few weeks, for that matter, to get away from his creditors who were beginning to press him uncomfortably close. And then there was Ulla. He almost wanted to believe in her virtue, her fidelity. Those thoughts brought him face to face with his dangerous projections of a month earlier: could he artfully be experiencing romantic love for the girl?

Fortuitously they got to his apartments before he could sink too deep into that abyss. He was scarcely surprised to see the building crowded with police, even less to find his luggage packed and waiting.

The rest was routine. He checked the windows, doors and desk out of habit, then whisked toward his apartment door with Schenley in tow. Now he was completely resigned to the idea of the trip but he felt it a matter of honor to continue the facade.

"Sergeant, I appreciate your concern, but you must understand that I owe it to my patients to be back in London within the week."

Schenley steered him toward the door, happy to go along with Whitcomb's deception.

"Of course, Doctor, all we ask is that you be with us till we break this case. I guarantee we'll have you back here within a few days." Schenley grinned in his most infectious manner, then he signaled to Peters to take Whitcomb's overnight case and the three left the apartments in good order.

On the elevator ride down to the lobby, Whitcomb permitted himself to be a bit more effusive. The Woosters, if he remembered correctly, had as neighbors a retired brigadier, his wife and four children. The oldest girl, when he last saw her, was abud with country air and sunshine. At seventeen, she'd be well equipped to brighten his stay in the Cotswolds.

"I do feel a bit like a Chief-of-State," he perked.

Schenley shrugged, anxious now to be rid of Whitcomb, who was getting to be quite a peacock. The thought that he'd have to spend the next several days with the man just entered his mind when the elevator stopped and the doors opened to reveal the hotel's small, but tastefully furnished lobby. They stepped out, he and Peters flanking Whitcomb, and began walking toward the large glassed entryway.

Whitcomb stopped for a moment and began fumbling about in his vest pocket.

"Forget something?" Schenley asked, anxious to get him into the limo outside.

"My lighter," he said.

At that moment, the air tore, shattered, fractured open with the sound of cracking glass. The air blurred in brief brilliance as a golden meteor flew from the shattered front window, through the lobby and straight into Whitcomb, its force carrying him back against the mirrored lobby wall, impaling him with an awesome, awful, pointed thud. The mirrored wall was pierced and cracked by the golden, brass-pointed projectile, now projecting from the small of its host's back. Underneath, on glass wall and black-tile floor, his blood ran with great and deadly speed, and he never had a chance to speak.

Chapter 15

DROPS of burning wax sizzled to the floor sending up curls of smoke. The blowtorch ate deeper into the likeness, the fire jet hissed and sputtered. Eyes, nose, chin and mouth curled and ran. Phibes bent closer to his work waving the sooty brass snout about the head like a sculptor. He chipped and drilled deeper with the jet, hissing as the features ran. He hissed and gouged the neck, hissed and seared the cheekbones, hissed again, and melted the brain pan.

Phibes cut the gas and threw the blowtorch onto a table cluttered with tools. Seven battered mounds now lined the circle of likenesses. Two masks of the Nurse, Miss Allan, and of Henri Vesalius, completed the circumference. Phibes eyed the lot, scowling and noticeably fatigued. Of course it was impossible to tell his precise mood because of the cosmetic nature of his features, but something could be divined about his inner attitude from his walk, his posture, his gestures. Observing Phibes was comparable to studying a blind man or a deaf-mute.

Nevertheless, the central question pressed urgent: what was known of Anton Phibes the man? He was first of all a generalist, a man equally at home with Kepler and Bach. That he was a patrician could not be determined simply because of his wealth but it is doubtful whether money or its absence would have changed him. He had ability, an iron character, resourcefulness, and the moral strength requisite to difficult judgments. He'd passed from the diffidence of his student days to the years of public service with ease and was able to accommodate the serenity of the former with the social prominence of the latter.

He was a man earmarked for brilliance but marked by tragedy. The love that gave him everything, took it all away. And, just as infinitesimal errors in the calibration of a telescope will preclude notice of an entire galaxy, Victoria's death devastated and subsequently dominated Phibes' life.

But others, it could be argued, endure tragedy without compounding it. Why not Phibes? He was a precise man, a man capable of infinite detail, of infinite patience. He had a strong sense of rectitude and an eye for the essential fact. As a physicist he had a primary concern with the general laws of motion, mass and time. He knew the importance of observation, was aware of Heisenberg's delineation of the effect of the observer on that which is observed. To this preoccupation with precision was added Phibes' practical knowledge of music. He was equally familiar with the classical treatment of rhythm and with Bartok's contemporary work in atonality.

Protean, logical, passionate, Phibes was a man who lived, who could live, on the grand scale. To find his specific reasons for turning to mass murder one would have to look to the man himself.

Phibes seemed terribly weary as he moved through the ballroom. Vulnavia, dressed now in a simple black dancer's costume, was dancing a stately pavanne to the accompaniment of the mechanical orchestra. He hardly bothered to notice as he took his seat at the rose-colored organ centered on a dais opposite the musicians. Vulnavia gazed at him trancelike, expecting him to play to her pavanne. Instead he initiated the floor elevator system and slowly sank into the shrine room on the level below.

Once inside that sepulchre Phibes' intense weariness seemed to soften. As his strong hands spanned the keys an image of Victoria appeared on a small projection screen mounted on the wall behind the organ. He glanced at her longingly; she'd been photographed at a spot along the Dover coast and stood alone on a crag with the surf awash and white far below. He pushed a stop on the keyboard, and soft seafoam sounds ensued as undercurrents to his music. Then another picture, a close-up of Victoria posed before some elms, appeared.

Phibes' eyes welled with tears as he played against a succession of portraits of his wife. She was in a skiff on the Thames, smartly dressed on a shopping excursion to Mayfair, at the breakfast table drinking from a tall white cup, running barefoot along a grass-matted river bank. Always in motion, charged with the energy of her youth and love, she was as near to Phibes as she had been then. Except. . . .

His voice filtered from a concealed speaker, metallic but

somehow touched with grace, as he read from John Donne's *The Good Morrow*

And now good morrow to our waking souls/which watch not one another out of fear;/for Love, all love of other sights controls.

He closed his eyes and increased the music's volume.

My face in thine eye, thine in mine appears/And true plain hearts doe in the faces rest/where can we find two better hemispheres/ without sharpe North, without declining West.

He bent his head lower to the keyboard as the words drew to conclusion. His strength was going fast.

Whatever dyes, was not mixt equally. If our two loves be one, or thou and I/Love so alike, that none doe slacken, none can die.

At that the last picture of Victoria faded, and Phibes ended his playing. The candles had burnt low and he sat in repose in the dark room, a brooding figure, permanently alone. In his hands he clasped a new brass ensign, an "arecha," the symbol for locusts.

As Phibes' strength wavered, Harry Trout, too, found himself wishing for more. The day had begun with a painfully strained briefing by Tom Schenley on the circumstances of Whitcomb's demise. So awkward and inexplicable was his murder, so sordid and crying for prevention were its circumstances, that Trout actually had to suppress an urge to laugh when the solemn Schenley unfurled the brass unicorn's head from its canvas wrappings and laid it on his desk. He hardly listened to Tom's description of the heavy rubber slingshot rigged like some medieval siege weapon on a rooftop across the street from Whitcomb's hotel, so impressed was he by the sleek lethal efficiency of the murder instrument.

Lunch had been steamed cod and biscuits followed by several straight Scotches, fortifications, he hoped, for his interview later with Audrey Basehart. He found himself recounting again the bare and baleful facts of the case, which was becoming more damnable by the hour, to the young woman whose persistence he couldn't help but admire. He'd already given her what little of Kitaj's effects they'd gathered from the wreckage and really had no reason to speak further but he couldn't refuse an interview. She was in complete control of her emotions that afternoon and seemed distinctly and pointedly interested in the progress of the case. After she left he credited to the depth of her affection a thought which was oddly disquieting.

The rest of the afternoon had been given over to a rigid review of the security preparations for the nurse and Vesalius. Miss Allan presented a special problem because she could not conveniently get away from her work. The hospital itself was large and rambling, with new wings and buildings complicating the floorplan. It would have been impossible to guard the myriad exits, ground level windows and elevators, so it was decided to concentrate on Miss Allan herself. She'd been provided with two bodyguards twenty four hours a day for the past four days. To add to the problem, Miss Allan's residence was in a rather new brick structure to the rear of the hospital opposite a small but heavily wooded park. She occupied an exterior room, and to shield her against an assault from the park, patrols were concealed in its thick undergrowth. In the building proper men were posted on both the 5th and 7th floors—her room was on the 6th floor—and at each exit.

Vesalius was another matter. He'd steadfastly refused to permit a guard in his home, claiming that it would cause him more discomfort than the protection was worth. Further, Vesalius persisted in his argument that he had been merely a consultant on the case and was not, in fact, a functioning member of the surgical team. Vesalius' interest in the case stayed high, and his development of the information on Phibes had been sufficiently helpful as to cause Trout to honor his request. Of course Whitcomb's death changed all that.

Trout was just in the process of ordering a guard for Dr. Vesalius when Sir John barrelled into his offices.

"Trout!"

The Inspector, accustomed to facing situations of the utmost desperation with a seasonal coolness, quaked inwardly. He'd been privy to the fact that a top level press conference had taken place somewhere upstairs earlier in the day.

"Trout, I have just spent twenty minutes of my time defending the honor, efficacy and, yes, even the professional capability of this department against the closest kind of questioning. It would not have been so attenuating but for the fact that the commissioners were there in person."

"Did they speak, sir?"

"Speak? Of course they spoke! They were in the thick of it. It got to the point where they were 'explaining' the presence of the Department!"

"That was most civic-minded of the commission."

"There'll be no witticism from this point on, Mr. Trout. The College of Surgeons is prepared to call for a parliamentary review, and they'll get one, too. But before that happens, I'll shake this department to the roots to get some appropriate action. Now, do you realize that we're in a crisis of the first magnitude?"

"The situation is critical, sir, but not desperate."

"Not desperate? One tenth of this department is now active on a case, looking for a man who, according to you, has been buried once."

"It's just a theory, sir."

"I don't know about your theories, Trout, but I've had a gut-full of your practice."

Trout got up and opened his office door. Crow continued his tirade unabated. "I'm talking to you. It seems to me that with immaculate precision you've been arriving on the scene just after the victim's death. This time, due no doubt to some organizational oversight, you arrive there *before* the crime. But as I've come to expect, that made little difference. It was still committed. A brass unicorn has been catapulted across a London street and impaled an eminent surgeon. Words fail me!"

Crow thundered out the door which Trout had held

open. Trout followed him and moved down the corridor in the opposite direction.

"Where are you off to now, Trout?"

"To the lavatory, sir." Would the man give him no peace?

"Highly appropriate! And then?"

"To the hospital to personally supervise the security measures. We'll be spending the night there."

"I expect some reassurances in the morning. And what of your prime suspect?"

"Dr. Phibes? Fragmentary information is all. The bank that closed his estate never saw him in person. Darrow, that music dealer, is steadfast in his claim to have seen the doctor, but he knows nothing else about him. Other than that we're sifting the files for psychopaths."

"Well, keep at it. And no more mishaps. As it is, I may have to review your position in the case."

"I understand, sir." Trout had heard these threats before. This seemed a bit stronger than in the past. Of course he knew that his job was on the line. But it was on the line every time he went out the door. He shrugged and hurried down the corridor.

When he got to the hospital it was already dark and the streets were unreasonably quiet, even though it wasn't yet 8:30. Trout had never liked hospitals, perhaps because he'd had the daylights scared out of him when, at age six, his parents had hospitalized him for a tonsillectomy and then neglected to visit him until after the operation. Later, they explained that they acted on the advice of the family doctor not to disturb his rest, but the terrors of that long night, filled with the comings and goings of the gurney in the hall, the clink of instruments, coughs, groans, wheezes, and the stink of ether, stayed with him.

He scanned the layout and was pleased with what he saw. The only evidence of the security force were two uniformed men, the regular patrolmen of the area, who were slowly moving in opposite directions from a deserted intersection at the far end of the square. The park was pitch black except for a dull glint of metal signifying the squad hidden there. Up above, on the main building's gabled roof, a lone figure stood in silhouette near a ventilator.

Vesalius met him at the door. As soon as they shook hands, Trout remembered he'd neglected to put a guard on the doctor. Now he'd have to keep Vesalius with him until arrangements could be made.

"Your office told me you'd be here, Inspector. As one of the principal players I thought it appropriate if I could be on hand when you talk to Nurse Allan."

Trout was pleased. "That was thoughtful of you, doctor. We're going to meet with her in the conference room downstairs." They passed a sergeant on guard at the elevator bank on their way to the stairwell. He snapped to attention as Trout passed.

"Everything quite normal, sergeant?"

"Nothing to report, sir."

They hurried down the steel stairs and through a long, green, pipe-lined corridor, entering the conference room at the end. Trout pointed to a large map of the hospital complex showing the multiplicity of its wings, outbuildings, laundry and boiler rooms, and he described the security measures to Vesalius.

"The whole place is completely sealed. Men from the Yard, as well as our locals, handpicked and briefed, are spotted at all the exits, on the roof, and in the park."

Vesalius watched intently as Trout traced the plan's details.

"We've got mobile units at every intersection. The main building has plainclothesmen on every floor, and her residence is sealed tighter than a drum. There are even some men on the roof to greet the bastard if he drops in on us via balloon—which I wouldn't put past him. I think she'll be all right."

Vesalius couldn't resist questioning him. "Just suppose Phibes is in the building now?"

"Was here before we got here, you mean?" Trout grinned. "Then we've got him. He can't get out. I hope he is, doctor,"

Vesalius wasn't amused. "After all, he has killed seven people in the last fourteen days."

They both turned to greet Miss Allan, a still attractive woman in her mid-thirties. Two plainclothesmen remained discreetly outside the room's windowed doors as she entered. She seemed pleased and relieved at seeing Vesalius.

"Doctor Vesalius, what on earth are you doing here? You're not involved in this charade are you?"

"In a sense, I'm afraid I am, nurse."

"But doctor, these men have told me I must not leave

the hospital grounds. And I did have plans to go to the theatre this evening. Why me? I mean that's surely not right. Can you tell me what's going on?"

Trout, seeing that she was becoming upset, urged her to retire. "Please Madam, would you be kind enough to go to your room; we'll have your supper sent up."

She bristled. "I've already eaten, thank you. Doctor?"

Vesalius looked at her intently. "I'm sorry, nurse. Inspector Trout is doing his best. You must go to your room and stay there, for the next twenty-four hours at least."

"But, doctor!"

"Please. I know what you must think, but the police have reason to believe that a man will try to kill you presently."

"*Kill* me? Whatever for?"

"It has to do with a case we served on, together with seven others, about four years ago. You and I are the only ones left alive."

"Victoria Phibes, yes, I read about it in the *Mail*. How awful." She was terribly shaken and started to sit down, but Trout and Vesalius, anxious to get her to the safety of her room, escorted her slowly up the elevator and tried to calm her fears. Guards were at each landing and a uniformed patrolman stood outside her room. They went inside with her, and Vesalius put water on for tea while Trout looked about the walls and windows. They left after further reassuring the frightened woman that they'd be in the building through the night, and that, by way of added precaution, the guard outside her door would check on her periodically. That seemed to assuage her and she promised to be off to sleep soon, having had enough excitement for one day.

When the two men left Nurse Allan's room it was a bit after eleven. Most of the night still lay ahead. They decided to continue their vigil by touring the rest of the layout. As they walked the crisply antiseptic corridors, Trout spoke with a bit of optimism.

"Don't worry, doctor. Sooner or later he's got to buck the oldest stone wall of them all— human error."

"If you believe that, Mr. Trout, you're giving the fiend a quality he's scarcely exhibited in our contact with him." Vesalius was rueful. "I'm afraid that if he's stopped by anything, it'll be by his own inflexible standards."

"How do you mean that?"

The two men passed the sentries who stood stiffly at the elevators. Vesalius persisted:

"Let's suppose that Phibes got out of that wreck alive. If he did, he would've been burned terribly or, equally terribly, injured—assuming he was thrown clear of the wreck before it exploded. He's probably as unrecognizable to himself as he is to others, with the exception of old Darrow, a condition which has only increased his grief. That, and the awful fact of his wife's death, is all that's kept him going in the years since. A continuity with only one theme: revenge. So far he's followed the classic pattern of the G'tach with precision."

"You're implying that he will not make a mistake."

"Remember he's a highly famed physicist. He's acutely

aware of errors in human calculation as well as their consequences. No, I'm afraid luck won't enter into it, Inspector. If we're to catch our man we must think quite precisely, quite mechanically. We will need to interrupt his process. Then, and only then, he becomes vulnerable."

While they thrashed about on the imponderables of their quarry, a white-garbed attendant rolled a tea wagon out of the seventh floor elevator, moved unmolested past the double guard, trundled the jangling cart down the long corridor and entered room #724, which was positioned directly over Nurse Allan's room on the floor below. Once inside, the man began pacing off certain measurements, marking off a large oblong on the wooden floor. Then he removed a small drill from the base of the tea cart and, bending to the work, proceeded to drill through the floor at a point directly in the center of the chalk oblong.

The drill pushed through. He removed it and squinted down through the hole. Pleased with what he saw, he unclasped a short rubber tube from a carboy on the undercarriage of the teacart, and after inserting the tubing into the hole, loosened a stopcock at the base of the carboy to send a green, treacly substance down the tube into the room below.

Elsewhere, Trout and Vesalius continued their lonely inspection.

"Three curses are left. Of course, doctor, there is the possibility that it might be your turn tonight."

Vesalius abandoned his cold rationale. "I've considered that over and over, but I have a feeling that I will be the last.

After all, I acted as a consultant in the case, not a participant. He may even overlook me entirely."

"And he may not. If he's going to follow the cycle, my friend, it will be darkness for you. And who knows what that will be." They rounded a corner, their voices trailing off. Two floors below Nurse Allan lay quite still under a thin syrupy layering of chlorophyll which inexorably oozed from the two-gallon carboy above. The soft flow had not been enough to awaken her from a sleep induced by sedatives, and she still breathed, though the thick layering would soon literally suffocate her if she didn't stir first.

To prevent that, Phibes released something else down the length of tubing: a horde of red army ants! The insects quickly covered the chlorophyll layering atop the sleeping Miss Allan. Green turned to black and then to red-black as the ants chewed their way first through the syrup and then, in a matter of a few seconds, through flesh and muscle.

She didn't have a chance to scream but died in the earliest moments of the invasion, in part by suffocation and in part by the carnivorous onslaught which had reached her major vessels before there was any possibility of response.

Then, as if to emphasize the destruction, Phibes let loose a swarm of locusts in fulfillment of the "arecha." Thousands of the green flying creatures shot out of the tubing and soon reduced the bed's occupant to skeleton, hopping and flying about in a terrible fury of destruction. They spared nothing: drapery was shredded, chairs gnawed to toothpicks, the couch was shredded to a lintball.

As this flurry of destruction was taking place, Trout and

Vesalius reached the first floor. They were still speaking of the remaining curses of the G'tach.

"What about the death of the first born? Have you considered that, doctor?"

"Indeed I have. I had an order brother but he's long dead, and I feel that that fact excludes me from this particular curse."

Trout pursued the logic. "Then you must resign yourself to the fact that I'm going to stay by your side until we finally apprehend this man. Of course, if your brother were still alive. . . ."

Then a new thought struck him: "What about *your* first born?"

Vesalius paled. "Lem! My God!" He ran toward the entrance.

Trout shouted to Schenley who was just then coming into the building. "Tom! Take the doctor home. Put a guard around his place, alert the local division and stay in contact with me."

Vesalius followed Schenley almost in a daze while Trout returned to his security check.

But its futility was now patent. Nurse Allan's room had been reduced to a shambles. Not a stick of furniture or shred of cloth remained. The entire room was eaten down to the metal behind the walls. Even the plaster had been eaten. A lone electric bulb swinging from the half chewed wires was the only remnant intact.

It flickered dimly.

Chapter 16

"OH, *No!*" The muffled shriek came from Doctor Vesalius' apartment. Trout heard it with apprehension as he waited for the elevator doors to open. Another shock right on the heels of Nurse Allan's death would be almost too much. Her room had literally been eaten down to the bare walls. Even the fixtures had gone before the swarm of locusts finally came to rest in a grey ball, twitching and lethal, above a window. He could only guess at the furious activity that had taken place in the room moments earlier. If the woman had offered any resistance it had been short and fruitless. Her skeleton, with a few locusts still caught in the dry hollows of the skull, was all that remained.

"No!"

Trout ran through the darkened apartment. Vesalius' train layout seemed untouched. The kitchen door stood ajar, sending a thin shaft of yellow light into the dining room. A few pillows had been thrown about, giving the room a dishevelled look; otherwise there were no signs of a struggle.

Trout ran upstairs. It was different there. A wall closet was open, its linens strewn over the floor. Both bedroom doors were ajar and Trout could see books and clothing jumbled about inside the room. He found Vesalius in Lem's room stiff with shock. The man's face was contorted in anguish, his hands were clenched, and his tie and collar, usually so neat, stood open in disarray. But Trout was most disturbed by the man's eyes, usually so calm and penetrating. They darted about now in a slow, wild, twitching fashion. Trout feared, the worst.

"He's gone!"

"Schenley told me. We'll do everything we can." The room showed little sign of violence. "A glass of brandy might do both of us good." He touched Vesalius very gently on the shoulder and motioned the doctor to join him downstairs. Trout didn't like the way Vesalius looked at all. Even in the softened parlor light the man was ashen, drained of all color. His reserve, his measured disdain, no longer served him and without defenses, the man appeared in danger of coming apart. Trout had seen the same phenomenon at work among the family or close friends of victims. The average person usually cried it out and then went into a shell, often helped along by a few drinks. Vesalius was another matter; other than his brilliance, his insistence on privacy, and his eclecticism, Trout knew virtually nothing about the man. He seemed to have no family or close friends, his son being his only companion. Trout couldn't guess the effect of the boy's loss.

Vesalius eased stiffly into the sofa while Trout fixed the

drinks. He stared, his eyes glassy, veiled. "How can it be?" he murmured, "how could I have known?"

The telephone rang.

Vesalius' face flickered with a mixture of fear and expectation. He moved quickly to answer it. "Yes?"

Organ music drifted out of the earpiece, swelled, then the phone went dead. Vesalius, visibly shaken, put the receiver softly into its cradle and started back to the couch. Trout finished decanting the brandy just as the phone rang again. He capped the bottle and picked up an extension as Vesalius answered a second time. The voice on the line was metallic and all too familiar. "Nine killed her, nine shall die," it said.

Vesalius shouted: "Is that Phibes? Phibes! *Phibes!*"

"Eight have died, soon to be nine. Nine eternities in doom."

It was confirmed now. Vesalius grew urgent. "Where are you Phibes? I must talk with my son. Where is my son? *Phibes!*" Vesalius fought for control.

"The organ plays till midnight on Maldine Square. Come alone." Then nothing. Vesalius hung up again, and glanced over at Trout, whom he seemed to recognize for the first time.

"I must go there. Perhaps he'll accept my life instead of my son's."

Trout could see he'd have to argue the man out of it. He wasn't prepared to give up another victim. "D'you think you can reason with a man of his stripe? If you do, you're as mad as he is. Dr. Phibes will have his appointment this evening, but with more company than he'd expected."

"You can't be serious, Inspector. You heard him. 'Come alone' were the instructions. The efforts of the police have caused him little discomfort thus far. Their pressure now will most certainly accelerate the death of my son."

Trout was adamant. "I'm sorry, doctor, but I cannot let you go there alone."

"But my son!"

"We'll take every precaution." Vesalius looked at him sullenly. "I'm prepared to stop you by force if necessary. I'm sorry, terribly sorry but *you* are my responsibility."

Vesalius' eyes narrowed. He turned away from Trout, his shoulders stooped in resignation. "Very well, Inspector. Whatever you say."

Trout, relieved that the standoff was over, turned to the telephone to organize the final assault on Phibes. He scarcely saw the blur to his left and had no time whatever to dodge the heavy chessboard which Vesalius brought down on his head. He crumpled to the floor.

Vesalius, now eager and full of purpose, quickly took his leave. "I'm sorry, too, Inspector, but my son is all that matters."

He closed the door very quietly. Trout, breathing evenly now, would be out for another hour at least.

Vesalius raced to his car, started it, and lurched away from the curb just as the policeman Trout had stationed at the building's entrance caught up with him. The poor man went sprawling as Vesalius pressed the accelerator to the floor.

His mind raced as he drove, trying to place Maldine Square. He knew it to be in Belgravia, but of its exact location he wasn't sure. In less than five minutes he had the Lagonda slicing through the sedate streets of the district, and in another minute he'd found Maldine Square, a cobbled enclosure channeled off the main roadway. An organ, towering up from a shuttered building taller than the others, marked the house as Phibes' own.

Vesalius parked the Lagonda on the outer road, ran the few steps along the cobbles and up the slate-tiered entrance to the mansion. The black oaken door had a brass marker shaped in the letter "P".

He banged on the door. It opened.

He was surprised to see the young woman who greeted him in an elaborate oriental robe and feathered headdress. He'd imagined Phibes lived alone.

He entered the hallway to the towering sounds of a fugue which streamed from the only lighted room on the floor. He went straight to the light and entered the long ballroom without introduction just as the music peaked.

The cloaked figure at the far end of the room brought the fugue to a close with a mass of chords. Finished, he rose from the instrument, turned and faced Vesalius. It was Phibes.

The man moved toward him, his carriage that of a host. Vesalius was forced to contain his own rage. "I've come for my son," he said.

"He will die at midnight."

"If you must take a life, take mine."

"I will have killed nine times in my life, Doctor Vesalius. How many murders can be attributed to you?"

Phibes had lessened the distance separating them with a stately, measured gait. The two men now stood facing each other, deadly adversaries and yet grim associates in that hour of their first meeting.

"I did not kill your wife."

"No?"

"I tried to save her."

Vesalius noticed the long cord in Phibes' neck. That explained his hollow, metallic speech. Further, Phibes' expression, save for his eyes, changed little during their conversation. Then it was clear that his features were artificial.

"You tried to save her . . .__with a knife in your hand."

Phibes tore the rubber base away from his face. Nothing was left beneath. The accident had taken his face, his personality, perhaps even his soul. He went on, the gross shriveled remnant of his face, giving brutal emphasis to his words. "You shall see your son, and under circumstances which may bring back memories to you, Vesalius."

Phibes moved to the wall near him, and reaching behind a curtain, activated the lights in a room below. The scene which was illuminated through the thick glass floor panels fully revealed Phibes' murderous inventiveness. The fiend had created an operating room, white tiled and brilliantly lit. On the long surgical table lay Vesalius' son, Lem, masked in sheeting, his head bound in bandages. Vesalius gasped.

"What is it you want?"

"The skill of your hands, Doctor. I'm giving your son the same chance that my wife had. You need not be alarmed; he has already been anesthetized."

Vesalius started forward, but Phibes restrained him, handing him over to Vulnavia who opened a trap door which led to the room below. Vesalius started down with the girl, then paused. "If anything happens to him I will kill you."

Phibes was imperious. "But you can't Doctor. I'm already dead."

Vesalius hurried down the short staircase to a small dressing room where, assisted by Vulnavia, he made himself ready as best he could.

At the same time Trout was groping about the darkened parlor of Vesalius' apartment in an effort to clear his head. Abruptly he remembered the preceding events, and grabbing his coat, dashed out to find Schenley, followed by a squad of men, just coming into the building. He grabbed Tom on the run and, giving him a quick summary of Vesalius' flight, set off for Maldine Square.

Vesalius entered the operating room, groping for the last reserves of his ability to guide him. A viewing panel lit up, illuminating an X-ray plate. Phibes' voice droned through a loudspeaker.

"An X-ray of your son's rib cage, Vesalius. You will observe that a tiny key has been lodged close to his heart. It will unlock the halter around your son's neck and free the trolley on which he rests."

Vesalius studied the plate, then looked over at the operating table as Phibes droned on.

"If you're wondering why you need to free the table, then I suggest you look above your son's head, Doctor."

Vesalius' eyes darted to the ceiling from which a large glass spiral tube coiled downward. As he watched, it dropped a few more inches, rotating like a snake ready to strike, finally coming to rest a few feet above his son's head. Phibes' voice went on evenly, precise and absolutely cruel in its absence of any modulation: "In a few moments acid will be released into that tube. Because of its viscosity it will move down slowly—but inexorably —to the lower outlet. In six minutes it will be directly over the boy's head. Exactly six minutes, doctor."

Vesalius was horrified. "For God's sake!"

"Oh don't cry upon God, Doctor Vesalius. He is on my side. He led me, showed me the way in my quest for retribution. Look not to God, Doctor, look to yourself, those hands, those skilled hands of yours. *You* can be the boy's only salvation. Look above him, Doctor."

Vesalius hurried into his gloves, helped by Vulnavia who then wheeled an instrument table into position. Phibes' voice continued:

"Did you know that my wife existed only six minutes on the operating table. Six minutes and she was dead. You murdered her."

Vesalius snarled through his mask as he selected his instruments. "No!"

"Murdered her. But you have what she did not: a

second chance. You must operate and remove the key, the key that will unlock the band around his neck. Six minutes, Doctor . . . six minutes. Perhaps your hands will shake and he will die under your knife, but six minutes is all you have."

Phibes' tirade had frozen Vesalius into immobility. He was trapped in the white, sterile silence of the operating room as the loudspeaker went dead, caught by the bitter extremity of his situation. Then the organ began, this time with the thin strains of a popular love tune. Still he did nothing.

"Doctor, Doctor!" Phibes said above the music. Vesalius looked up. "The acid has started to descend."

Vesalius fought his inaction for another agonizing second, then turned to his son and prepared to operate. His gloved hands moved into the prescribed, deliberate patterns, preparing the surface of the chest at a point just below the heart, where Phibes had lodged the key. "I leave you to your operation, Doctor," the fiend said. "I know surgeons require the utmost concentration, especially in circumstances like this. Vulnavia and I will be watching."

Vesalius made the first incision: the solution was now in his hands.

In the ballroom upstairs Phibes was preparing for a conclusion of another kind. He played an overture while Vulnavia moved about the room ripping curtains, tipping over furniture, and tearing the lights from the walls. Phibes' music kept pace with the girl's furious activity. It seemed rehearsed, a prelude to something larger.

Vesalius was too busy to be bothered with the crashing overhead. He worked at a heightened pace, a pace sustained only by his great skill and control. He'd gotten past the outer layer of skin, which was now held back by a large retractor, and was slicing the fascia over the rib cage. He mopped feverishly with a wad of sponge, placed a few hemostats to control the bleeding, and then grabbed the bone saw to break into the thoracic cavity.

The acid was halfway down the glass helix!

Phibes, his head back in perverse rapture, played the organ at full volume. Behind him the ballroom was in a shambles. The crystal lamps lay smashed on the floor. The drapery had either been pulled down, or hung against the Casino Royale backdrop in forlorn shreds. Two of the three overhead chandeliers were also down, smashed to bits on the floor. The other had been broken where it hung: only one large electric bulb glowed through the shards of glass which remained. The large ballroom, once so ornate, was now in ruins.

But despite that, Phibes seemed pleased as he pedalled and played the heavy strains, sneaking a glance now and then at Vulnavia who had started on the wainscotting along one wall and was stripping it off, piece by piece. The puppet orchestra, their tuxedos flecked by bits of plaster and glass, sat in a comic expressionless patience.

Vesalius finished sawing and gingerly bent back the eighth and ninth ribs to reveal the small heart pulsing regularly. The sight of it charged his own resolve. He seized a probe and began the search for the key. It took a few tense seconds before he found it.

The acid had inched well past the halfway point. Vesalius would still have to remove the key, which was lodged beneath the heart, before he could free the table.

Phibes observed his efforts through the glass panel above. He saw Vesalius locate the key, drew back when the probe made contact, then glowered triumphantly when he lost it. Vesalius reached deep into the thorax below the heart. Finally he had the key; it was out; he was holding it in his hand. The acid seeped closer. Would it be close enough? Phibes tensed expectantly.

Suddenly a heavy hammering shook the front door. Phibes' eyes shot toward the hallway, then back to Vulnavia. At a signal she drew a pearl-handled revolver from her belt and fired at the tall mirrors above the ruined wainscotting.

The banging grew louder, loud enough to shake the entire house. The wooden shutters at a side window vibrated, then splintered, the glass beneath shattered by a crowbar.

Vulnavia turned her attention to the remaining chandelier. She fired once, twice, the second bullet brought the heavy crystal plummeting to the floor.

Just before the crystal fell, Phibes saw Vesalius fit the key into the locked hasp about Lem's neck. The metal parted. He rolled the heavy table to the side, just as the acid dripped to the floor with an angry sizzle.

The ballroom was suddenly cast into semi-darkness. Phibes quickened his tempo as the police, Harry Trout at the lead, kicked away the remaining pieces of shutter at the far end of the ballroom.

Incongruously, the orchestra started up, playing a somewhat out of time accompaniment to Phibes at the organ.

"Phibes! It's Phibes!" Trout shouted. His men crouched, and started to close the distance, their clubs drawn. Trout and Schenley led the advance with heavy flashlights. Then a large couch hurtled across the floor, partly blocking their way. Vulnavia stood in the center of the floor brandishing a large axe. The orchestra played at a frenzied pace.

For a moment they were at a standoff. Then Trout parried by rolling the couch back, forcing Vulnavia toward the dais. In the confusion Phibes had activated the lift and was sinking to the level below. To cover his retreat, Vulnavia backed through the musicians, whose movements had become erratic, and took up a position next to the organ. She would protect her master to the end.

The squad reached the stage. One policeman got his leg up on the dais to go after Phibes, but was sent back sprawling by a terrific clout from the saxophone player. The others tried, but met similar fates from the frenzied musicians who flailed and swung their instruments with senseless violence.

Trout and Schenley worked their way around to the side. They had to get to the organ before it disappeared.

At that the band stopped. Instruments clattered to the floor and the musicians came to rest. The organ, which had continued playing during the descent, now drew closer. Then it rose up from the floor. Vulnavia, her back to Trout and Schenley, was at the keyboard. Before they could reach her she rose and, grasping a slender dagger from near the keys, plunged it into her side. Schenley rushed to her but it was too late. The haunted girl died as she had lived, without a word passing her lips.

It all happened in an instant but it was long enough for Phibes to reach the shrine room. Once safely inside, a calmness smoothed the despair that had distorted his features for so long. His movements were gentle, almost affectionate as he made his way to a small chamber. There he pulled away a gauze diadem and gazed on his wife's body, which lay, perfect in every way, in a large double quartz coffin.

He sighed and climbed in beside her. Then, with an expression of thankful repose on his brow, he adjusted a tube containing embalming fluid to his arm and closed his eyes for the last time.

Upstairs Trout and Schenley pulled Vulnavia's form from the organ and after searching a bit, found the key to the elevator mechanism. As they rode down to the next level, they were greeted by an exhausted but much relieved Vesalius.

The three men searched the lower level, finding nothing but barren brick walls.

"He's gone, vanished, and that's impossible," Schenley said.

Vesalius shook his head. "But that still leaves the final curse."

Trout shrugged. "We'll not see the last of Dr. Phibes

until the tenth curse. I suggest we be thinking about that, gentlemen."

Stay tuned - more Dr. Phibes coming soon!
Dr. Phibes The Real Androbots©

Featuring more of
'Sophie'

The newest of the wondrous
Clockwork Wizards©

Like" + "Share"

"THE CULT-CLASSIC DR. PHIBES SERIES"

on Facebook:

https://www.facebook.com/DrPhibesVulnaviasSecret
https://www.facebook.com/DrPhibesInTheBeginning
https://www.facebook.com/DrPhibesRisesAgain
http://www.facebook.com/pages/Dr-Phibes/189893094376380

Visit our blog:

http://authorized-dr-phibes-blog.blogspot.com/

The AUTHORIZED DR. PHIBES BLOG by the author of
'THE CULT-CLASSIC DR. PHIBES SERIES'

Visit and watch our Youtube Channel:

FOREVER PHIBES VIDEO CHANNEL

http://www.youtube.com/user/FOREVERPHIBES

"THE CULT-CLASSIC DR. PHIBES SERIES"

Visit + Like + Share
"Dr. Phibes" on Facebook today and
become a Dr. Phibes Phan Forever.

http://authorized-dr-phibes-blog.blogspot.com/
https://www.facebook.com/DrPhibesVulnaviasSecret
https://www.facebook.com/DrPhibesInTheBeginning
https://www.facebook.com/DrPhibesRisesAgain
http://www.facebook.com/pages/Dr-Phibes/189893094376380

– ATTENTION ALL DR. PHIBES PHANS –

ORIGINAL DR. PHIBES SERIES BOOK COVERS

THE CULT-CLASSIC *DR. PHIBES SERIES*

NEW DR. PHIBES SERIES
COLLECTORS BOX-SET SPECIAL EDITION BOOK COVERS

NOW *EXCLUSIVELY* AVAILABLE
- ONLY THROUGH OUR -
AUTHORIZED DR. PHIBES BLOG:

http://authorized-dr-phibes-blog.blogspot.com/

Buy and read all four today and become a Dr. Phibes Phan
Forever!

THE CULT-CLASSIC *DR. PHIBES SERIES*

WILLIAM I. GOLDSTEIN is the creator of **DR. PHIBES** and the best selling author of **THE CULT-CLASSIC DR. PHIBES SERIES** including **DR. PHIBES, DR. PHIBES RISES AGAIN!, DR. PHIBES IN THE BEGINNING,** and the just recently published **DR. PHIBES VULNAVIA'S SECRET.** He is also co-writer of the top grossing horror motion picture **THE ABOMINABLE DR. PHIBES**, starring Vincent Price. The classic horror film has just been re-released in the United States on Blu-Ray as part of The Vincent Price Collection. William Goldstein lives in Los Angeles and is currently busy collaborating with his son **Damon J. A. Goldstein** on **BOOK IV of THE CULT-CLASSIC DR. PHIBES SERIES; DR. PHIBES THE REAL ANDROBOTS.**

For more information about
Dr. Phibes and The Cult-Classic Dr. Phibes Series
contact
foreverphibes@earthlink.net

TEN CURSES OF DEATH

The doctors of London were being murdered —horribly, grotesquely, monstrously. The first was stung to death by bees; the next was torn to bits by bats. The third was mutilated with the mask of a frog. The fourth was savagely drained of all his blood.

Somehow the deaths seemed to follow a fiendish pattern, all part of a bizarre ritual based on the ten curses of the Old Testament —*boils, bats, frogs, blood, rats, beasts, locusts, hail, death of the first born...and darkness.*

No one knew why.

No one could stop them.

No one, that is, except Dr. Phibes—a half-dead madman with a horrific master plan that had only just begun....

DON'T MISS THIS SPINE-SEARING FILM

James H. Nicholson and Samuel Z. Arkoff present

VINCENT PRICE • JOSEPH COTTEN
IN
"DR. PHIBES"
Also Starring
HUGH GRIFFITH and TERRY-THOMAS
Presenting
VIRGINIA NORTH as VULNAVIA
Written by
James Whiton and William Goldstein
Produced by
Louis M. Heyward and Ronald S. Dunas
Executive Producers
Samuel Z. Arkoff and James H. Nicholson
Directed by Robert Fuest
An American International Picture
Color by Movielab

ORIGINAL "DR. PHIBES" BOOK I MOVIE TIE-IN BACK COVER
PUBLISHED BY AWARD BOOKS 1971

www.ingramcontent.com/pod-product-compliance
Lightning Source LLC
Chambersburg PA
CBHW072243020325
22838CB00012B/875